THE Romeo AND Juliet CODE

by **PHOEBE STONE**

Arthur A. Levine Books

AN IMPRINT OF SCHOLASTIC INC.

Library of Congress Cataloging-in-Publication Data

Stone, Phoebe, 1947–
    The Romeo and Juliet code / by Phoebe Stone. — 1st ed.
        p. cm.
    Summary: During World War II, eleven-year-old Felicity is sent
from London to Bottlebay, Maine, to live with her grandmother, aunt,
uncle, and a reclusive boy who helps her decode mysterious letters
that contain the truth about her missing parents.
    ISBN 978-0-545-21511-4 (alk. paper)
    [1. Identity — Fiction. 2. World War, 1939–1945 — United
States — Fiction. 3. Families — Fiction. 4. Ciphers — Fiction.
5. Maine — History — 20th century — Fiction.] I. Title.
    PZ7.S879Ro 2011
    [Fic] — dc22

                                                            2010030005

10 9 8 7 6 5 4   12 13 14 15

Printed in the U. S. A.   23

Book design by Whitney Lyle

First edition, January 2011

For my father,
who stayed behind in England so many years ago

I was always told that my dad, Danny, loved danger. I was told that he was a bit reckless and daring. And that's just the way he pulled the car up into the sandy driveway at my grandmother's house in Maine. We could see the ocean below us crashing and pounding against the jagged rocks. Danny seemed to put the brakes on just at the edge of the cliff.

My mum, Winnie, reached out and touched his arm gently and we sat there in silence for a moment while Danny took a deep breath. "Shall we carry on, then?" said Winnie, looking round to the backseat at me. "Felicity, shall I bring Wink up to the porch?"

Even though I was eleven years old, I was still quite attached to Wink. I was most dreadfully embarrassed about it and hoped no one my age here in America would ever find out that I still loved a big, brownish, cheerful British bear. The thing about Wink was, he always smiled, even at the edge of a cliff.

Danny got out of the car and started for the house with my suitcases. He took the path through wild rosebushes because he knew the way. After twelve years of being in England, my Danny was coming home. I had never been here before and neither had my mum, Winnie. Winnie kept saying, "Danny, you should have told us how lovely it all is. Felicity, isn't it lovely! Look at the sky." She got out of the car, and the veil on her hat blew across her face. Her white linen dress billowed in the wind. She put her arm over my shoulder and we followed Danny along the path towards the old house that seemed to loom at the highest point along the coast.

Uncle Gideon, whom I had never met before, stood on the long wraparound porch and didn't say anything much when we walked towards him. His hands seemed large at his sides, and I noticed he was frowning and shifting his weight back and forth from one foot to the other.

Then Winnie's hat blew off in the wind and went dropping down the long steps towards the sea. Uncle Gideon saw the hat go rolling off and he rushed down the steps, slipping on the last one and stumbling in the sand, but he caught the hat. Then he came huffing and puffing back up to the porch. His hair was all blown about and his face was terribly red. But when he handed the hat back to Winnie, he looked away, and when she talked to him, he wouldn't answer her.

My dad, Danny, reached out to shake hands with Gideon, who was his brother, but Gideon seemed unable to move. He stood there frozen as if he'd just been shot. Then Danny lunged towards Gideon and tried to hug him, but Uncle Gideon pushed him away and shook his head. Danny finally slapped one arm across Uncle Gideon's back. And as they stood there staring out at the water, I saw Danny slip a small box into Uncle Gideon's jacket pocket.

"Felicity darling," said Winnie, with pearly drops of water on her cheeks, "this is your uncle Gideon. Yes, it is. There he is. Run and give him a great hello."

On the whole, British children are very forgiving and proper and I was trying to be so, but secretly, very secretly, I was thinking, *If Uncle Gideon has been angry with Winnie and Danny, then I shall be angry with Uncle Gideon.* Suddenly looking at me, Uncle Gideon got terribly apologetic and he tried to pat me on the top of my head and act all chummy in a very awkward way.

I took two tiny steps backwards and I said, "Hello," looking down at my feet. I had a hole in the bottom of one of my shoes and there was sand on the porch and I was letting the sand seep into my shoe, trying to collect as much as I could under my toes.

My grandmother stood in the hallway. Her face was

behind the mesh of the screen door, all shadowy and silent. She did not come out of the house.

Just for balance, I held on tight to my bear, Wink. I held on because it felt a bit like the wind might sweep us all off the porch and away into the dazzling white American clouds. It felt like the wind might sweep us all off the porch and away into the blue ocean sky that seemed to pitch this way and that with the sound of the roaring sea crashing against the rocks below us, over and over again.

★ *Two* ★

I always called my mum Winnie and my dad Danny. I
never called them Mum and Dad as other children do.

"Is that the British way?" asked Uncle Gideon, picking up a shell and holding it out in front of me in his
large palm. I thought his hand was shaking ever so
slightly. "Is that the way they say it over there?"

"No actually," I said, rolling my eyes away, trying
not to look at him or the shell. I was wondering what
terrible things had happened in the past that had caused
everyone to seem so uncomfortable. And besides, I was
trying not to cry because Winnie and Danny had just
pulled away in that car without a roof. Winnie's hat was
tipped to one side, her veil blowing out behind her. Danny
was in a white linen suit as well, with his silk necktie
fluttering in the wind. They beeped the horn as they
disappeared down the road and I could still hear it in
my mind.

"Just as if they're going off to be married again. It's
so romantic," whispered Aunt Miami to me. She had
stayed in the hallway with my grandmother while they

were here, but in the end she had rushed out to hug Danny good-bye. "Did you see how he held her hand the whole time? Does he often do that?"

I would always remember Winnie and Danny like · that, in a wash of sunlight, veiled and waving, the ocean behind them and beyond the ocean, Britain, England, my true home.

As I walked back towards the house with Aunt Miami, Uncle Gideon tried to interest me in several more seashells, but my eyes were all blurry. I actually only cried about five teardrops. I was counting them to keep the sadness away. I found out that one eye cried more than the other eye, or else a few tears got away without being accounted for.

★ ☆ ★

In the dark hallway, my grandmother (everybody called her The Gram) looked at Uncle Gideon and said, "Have they gone?"

And Gideon nodded. The Gram closed her eyes and leaned her head against the brown wallpaper. Then she popped them open and said, "Well, after all these years, I meet my granddaughter! And how do you do! I see she has the true Bathburn forehead."

"I *am* half Budwig," I said quite loudly. "My mum, Winnie, keeps her maiden name. And I am called Felicity Bathburn Budwig."

Then my grandmother whispered something in Gideon's ear and he said, "Oh. Um, of course. Well, shall I show you where your room is and all that?"

I tried not to answer, but in the end I said, "Yes," in a very solemn way. And I climbed the long stairs behind my uncle Gideon.

As I climbed those long dark stairs, so began my stay in Bottlebay, Maine, USA, where they didn't have tea at night, they had supper, and no one said "jolly good" or "jolly right" or "I should think so, shouldn't I." Instead, they said "super!"

"Oh, that's super," said Uncle Gideon with one suitcase in each hand, looking nervously back at me over his shoulder to check that I was still there.

That was after I had said, "I think I am going to be staying here a while because there's a war in England and a lot of the buildings are being bombed to pieces."

Uncle Gideon said again, "Super! Oh, I don't mean about the buildings, but super about your being here, staying here. We live on a sandy point which is unusual for this part of Maine. A lot of people like the ocean generally. I mean, sometimes they pay oodles of money to stay near it. I mean, do you like the sound of the sea? Maybe? Sort of?"

"No," I said, "it's a very lonesome sound, isn't it."

Uncle Gideon turned his head away from me then, as if he was trying suddenly to hide his face.

We were now up one flight. There were some bedrooms off the long hall and we passed a closed door near the landing. I was feeling ever so tired from the long stairs, so I stopped for a moment. Uncle Gideon said, "Wait. No. I mean, oops, would you mind staying away from that door over there? Could you kind of steer clear of it for me?"

"Oh," I said, "sorry."

"Well, now, about your aunt Miami," Uncle Gideon said, clearing his throat. "Her room is just across the hall here. She loves flowers. Look at all the bouquets she's got in there. And I'll tell you something while she's downstairs, to get things straight from the start. We are the Bathburns of Bottlebay. And your aunt Miami's real name is Florence Bathburn, but she changed it a while back to Miami. And you can see why, being as she is a young woman and living way out here on the point on the ocean...Florence Bathburn sounded boring and old maid-ish, but Miami has a lot of pizzazz. Don't you think?"

"I should think so," I said.

"Oh, you should, should you?" said Uncle Gideon. "Now, don't stop here. We've got to lug these suitcases up and around one more time to the third floor."

I looked back at the door I was not to go near. It looked like a perfectly ordinary dark wooden door. I thought about The Gram standing in the shadows in the hallway. She didn't come out to kiss my Winnie and Danny. Why didn't she kiss them and hug them?

"Yes, this house gets blown about pretty badly now and again in the weather. But we usually stay put during storms. We Bathburns take pride in the fact that we have never gone to the shelter in town during a hurricane. Not once," said Uncle Gideon, taking a deep breath and then looking over at me out of the corner of his eye.

Why did The Gram stay in the hallway? Why did Uncle Gideon push Danny away when he tried to hug him? How long would Winnie and Danny be gone?

I tried not to say one more word. I pretended my mouth was sewn shut like Wink's. I was practically strangling that poor bear right now, my arm was so tight round his neck.

"So, what do you think? Do you like the house?" said Uncle Gideon in a hopeful, rather sheepish way. He closed his eyes and put a hand over his face and then he opened one eye and peeked at me through two of his fingers while he waited for my answer.

"Well," I said finally, "it is rather tall, isn't it."

"It's what you call a Victorian," he said. "It was built in 1850. Hasn't been touched since. But that's no fault of mine. I guess we should get rid of some of the old Victorian furniture, but we're used to it here. It's cozy and lived in. Every year, Miami threatens to tear down the old wallpaper and put up something with some pizzazz. But The Gram won't let her, because The Gram runs things around here. You'll find that out.

"Now, what we've got here," Uncle Gideon said, opening a short door at the top of the last flight of stairs, "is a little tower room we call the widow's peak. Look at the height and the views and see the little porch around the outside? That's called a widow's walk. This was once a sea captain's house, and his wife would stay up here to watch for his sailing ship to come over the horizon. All the families along the shore here waited for ships to come home. A lot of them never came back, you know."

Once inside the room, there were many windows to the ocean, and I could see the hill behind the house, covered in scrub grass and tangled trees and wild rosebushes, and there was a small road leading away over the hill. I looked out on that small road, hoping to spot Winnie and Danny's car, but by then, it was already long gone.

"This will be your room in a temporary sort of way, I guess," Uncle Gideon said, frowning again and then pinching the bridge of his nose very tightly with his thumb and fingers. "Do you hear the wind? It talks to you up here all the time. Sometimes it moans, some-times it calls, sometimes it sings. Do you like the sound of the wind? A little bit?"

"No," I said. I was hoping to say only words like *yes* and *no* to Uncle Gideon whenever possible.

"Oh, we Bathburns love the sound of the wind. Every one of us, even The Gram. Perhaps it's because out here the wind is all we have."

I wondered then why my grandmother was called The Gram, but I soon got used to it. Just as I grew used to the constant sound of the sea and the tide crashing against the rocks, and the wet, damp smell of seaweed and salt and the forever-calling seagulls and the wind.

★ Three ★

The next day, the sky darkened to a miserable gray, and endless sheets of rain fell and the ocean tossed about like something terrible and unhappy and restless. I had nothing to do but walk here and there, looking at the house. The dining room and sitting room at the front were dark, or at least there were long velvet curtains covering the windows, so you could hear the ocean all round you, but you couldn't see it unless you peeked through the curtains, which I did. I stood behind them, looking down and out at the water and the rain. I was standing there missing Winnie and Danny. I was writing a letter to them, leaning my paper against the window, watching the rain blur over the glass.

> *Dear Winnie and Danny,*
> *I miss you already. You didn't exactly tell me*
> *when you are coming back. What does "soon"*
> *mean? I do wish you wouldn't go home to London,*
> *because of the war and the bombs and all that. I*
> *know you said not to send letters to our flat*

*because they wouldn't get through and to keep
them in a box until you get back, but I should like
to post this letter. Where should I send it? There's a
telephone on the landing here, but no one uses it.
Will you ring me up? Please?*

Love,
Felicity

*P.S. To be cheerful, I should say I've been
putting my hair in plaits, as usual. I've started
calling them braids like you do, Danny. So far I've
been hearing a lot of Danny words like flashlight
and antsy. The Gram asked me yesterday if I've
always been antsy by nature. Have I?*

I wasn't hiding, honestly, because British children on
the whole never hide or snitch or lie, but it turned out
no one knew I was behind the curtains. I was terribly
sorry to be sneaking about by mistake. Quite by accident
I heard The Gram say to Uncle Gideon in the hall, "So
how are you holding up with the child being here?"

"Oh, I guess I feel like I'm being ripped to pieces,"
said Uncle Gideon.

"Well, you better take this tray up to Captain Derek
before she comes downstairs."

I stood there ever so quietly behind the curtains, trying not to snore or sneeze or cry, hoping I wouldn't get hiccups, thinking to myself, *Ripped to pieces because of me? And who is Captain Derek? Is there an old sea captain hidden away somewhere upstairs? Why didn't Winnie and Danny tell me?*

I pressed myself against the window until Uncle Gideon had gone upstairs, with the dishes clattering on the breakfast tray, and The Gram had disappeared into the back rooms behind the kitchen. How could Winnie and Danny have left me here with an uncle who was angry with them and a sea captain I knew nothing about tucked away somewhere in the house and a door I had to steer clear of and a sky that only rained?

I folded the letter and put it in my pocket and I went out into the hall and I opened the front door. I looked far off and away where the edge of the sky touched the water. Everything was all clouded and darkened and blurry with rain.

"Oh, *there* she is," said The Gram. "You scared us. We didn't know where you were." I turned round, and The Gram and Aunt Miami were standing there behind me. Gideon was bringing the breakfast tray back downstairs, the toast and eggs on the plate, untouched. Gideon was so tall, with a great bunch of reddish-brown hair, and for some reason that made me notice his eyes. I tried to avoid them, but they seemed to be everywhere, watching me.

On the whole, I am quite shy until you get to know me and then, Winnie says, I can be rather "rambunctious," whatever that means. I do try to be very proper the way my Winnie always said I ought to be, though sometimes I can't keep myself quiet. Sometimes, whatever it is that wants to pop out of my mouth goes right ahead and pops. "Excuse me," I said. "I'm frightfully sorry, but is there a captain of some sort upstairs somewhere?"

Uncle Gideon looked at me with sorry surprise then, as if I were a glass jar he had just dropped and broken by mistake.

Aunt Miami bit her lower lip. She was clutching a little book against her heart and wearing a lovely, soft, silk party dress. She seemed always to be ready to attend a party.

The Gram looked at Aunt Miami and then at Uncle Gideon. Their eyes all went round and round to each other and then back to me, like bumblebees stuck on the wrong side of the window glass, knocking against the same useless spot over and over again.

Then finally, Uncle Gideon said, "Um, well, yes, um,

actually, Captain Derek is here." He cleared his throat again. "Somewhere."

"Oh, he'll be coming out of his room soon," said Aunt Miami.

"Perhaps he'll be down for dinner," said The Gram. "Of course, he will."

"Or breakfast tomorrow," said Uncle Gideon, nodding his head up and down. Then The Gram pushed her face into Uncle Gideon's large shoulder, and he patted her hair gently and shut his eyes very tightly.

I put my hand on the letter in my pocket. I didn't know how to send it, but I was not going to cry. I decided to look up at the ceiling, hoping to find something terribly interesting up there that would help. But ceilings never offer any assistance. They are usually very plain. This one was dark and too far away to see anything except shadows. I decided I was not going to talk anymore at all. I turned round completely so I was facing the wall.

"Never mind about Derek for just now," said Uncle Gideon. "The Gram has made muffins this morning. Haven't you, Mother?"

"Oh, well, have you ever tasted one of The Gram's muffins?" asked Aunt Miami.

"Oh," said Uncle Gideon, "there's no other word to describe them. *Ohhhh* is the perfect word. Won't you come and try one? Please?"

When I finally did turn back round, Uncle Gideon was looking at me with his brown eyes tilted down. Then he wiped his face nervously with a handkerchief. "They're made with almonds and a secret ingredient that The Gram won't divulge. She won't tell a soul, not even the president of the United States."

"That's right," said The Gram.

"Please?" Uncle Gideon said again.

"Very well, then. I'll try one bite," I said, looking up the long stairs for a sign of Captain Derek. But all I saw were endless steps going round and up, round and up to the next floor, and then beyond to my windy tower room at the top of the house.

Aunt Miami went over to the open door and leaned her head against the screen, looking out at the slapping, wet, rainy, gray sea. She sighed and then she opened her book and started reading aloud, "*O Romeo, Romeo, wherefore art thou Romeo. Deny thy father and refuse thy name, or if thou wilt not, be but sworn my love, and I'll no longer be a Capulet.* Isn't it a lovely passage?" she said. "So poetic, so dreamy."

"There she goes again," said Uncle Gideon. "She's rather stuck on that play, in my opinion. Shall we have our muffins, then?"

I did finally go into the kitchen, but only because I *had* to.

Most British children generally believe that all Americans wear cowboy hats and cowboy boots and ride horses about and like to shoot at things. I hadn't expected Americans to be like this. I don't think any British child would have liked the Bathburns (myself included). They were too big and strange and sad. Well, Uncle Gideon was, anyway. And I hadn't expected to be in such a dark house with an unseen sea captain roaming about and no mailing address for my precious Winnie and Danny.

And so it was on that very first miserable, wet morning in Bottlebay, Maine, USA, that I took a bite of The Gram's secret almond and honey muffins. And I had to close my eyes afterwards, to keep my British balance. I tried not to say anything, but that didn't seem to matter.

"What did I tell you?" said Uncle Gideon.

"See what we meant?" said Aunt Miami.

"Well, that settles it," said The Gram. "She must have a nickname. Everybody gets a nickname here if they like my muffins. What about Flissy? We'll drop the

Budwig part altogether for now, if that's all right with you. You really can't go around with a great big, long name like Felicity Bathburn Budwig."

"Flissy Bathburn is better," said Aunt Miami. "It's got more pizzazz."

"What do you say, Fliss?" asked Uncle Gideon, tilting his head in a shy way. He backed up and knocked over a plant on the edge of the kitchen counter. Then he put on a fake British accent and said, "Jolly good, eh?"

I didn't answer him. I wasn't sure at all how I felt about being Flissy Bathburn. Finally, I said, "Perhaps we should ask my Danny what he thinks first."

"Oh, I see," said Uncle Gideon, looking down. "Of course. Really. No. Fine. Of course."

But I had a feeling it was no use. Sometimes pet names stick and sometimes they don't. Flissy seemed to stick instantly and I was instantly stuck with it. I could just tell. I knew it.

★ *Four* ★

I heard no more about Captain Derek. I saw nothing of him anywhere in the house, and I had a chance that rainy afternoon to poke about the whole dark place. On the dining room table was the day's newspaper, dated May 25, 1941. On the front page I read, "The British sea giant, the largest warship in the world, the HMS *Hood* was blown to bits yesterday in the waters between Iceland and Greenland by the new German battleship, the *Bismarck*." It went on to say that the war in Europe was still raging and that the bombing in London by Nazi planes had grown worse that month. I sat down and put my head on the table and cried. I knew Danny's work was terribly important and I knew Winnie had to be with him. But why did they go back to London with all the bombing?

I had pulled Wink out of bed earlier. He had been, as Americans say, "taking it easy" up in my room. I meant not to carry him about so much. Even my teacher in London had been alarmed when my mum mentioned in a teacher's conference that I still carried Wink about.

"You haven't let go of your old bear yet at eleven years old?" she said to me. "Not a good sign. Not at all. Not at all." And then she shook her head at Winnie and wrote something in her notebook.

I hugged Wink over and over again now. I kissed his ears, which always made me feel better because his ears were still deliciously soft. I kept thinking about that box my Danny had slipped into Uncle Gideon's pocket. It couldn't have been a box of sweets, because why would he make a secret of that? And everyone here seemed always to be whispering together and nodding towards me. The Gram cried a bit, and Uncle Gideon was overly jolly and bumped into things, knocking vases and cups over by mistake, and Auntie read all the time and didn't talk much, and then, suddenly, they all seemed to disappear, leaving me to wander about alone.

I went upstairs to look at the door I was to steer clear of. I must confess I put my head ever so lightly against it, trying to hear a sound coming from within. Perhaps all I heard was the ocean. I wondered if Captain Derek was in there. I pictured his old matted beard and his long, white tangled hair.

I looked in the other doors down the hall as they were all standing open. There was Uncle Gideon's messy bedroom in front, with a full view of the sea.

Newspapers and books were all over his bed and on the floor. Across the hall was The Gram's tidy room, which smelled of lilac soap. And then there was Auntie Miami's room with a Clark Gable signed photograph taped to her mirror. Yesterday she had said she mails away coupons and gets back photos of movie stars signed "*To Miami Bathburn with love.*" (Uncle Gideon had called it "a poor substitute for a social life." Auntie swatted at him with her book when he said that.)

Across and down the hall from the door I was to steer clear of was another dark wooden door where another bedroom ought to have been. I wasn't told to stay away from that door, so I turned the knob ever so carefully. But I found the door was locked.

Finally, I took Wink back up to my room. He was certainly a bear that preferred to be lying down rather than being dragged about by his soft ears. He needed time to adjust, to think. He hated being moved about constantly, and I knew he hated it here. Wink was not a suspicious bear at all, but he felt Uncle Gideon was *too* interested in him and quite secretive about something. And so was The Gram. All this led Wink to be slightly suspicious. Uncle Gideon had said things in his fake British accent like "What ho, Wink! Enjoying yourself? Not a bad old place here, what?" And he squeezed Wink's nose and kept babbling on at him even when it was quite clear that Wink was not going to answer him. He was a British bear after all and he did not wish to become American. And anyway, Wink loved Danny very much and had no room in his small bear's heart for someone who was angry with Danny.

I sat on the bed in my widow's peak room. I could see and feel the ocean all round me. It seemed as if I was in a lonely boat cast off to sea all by myself. I was quite used to loneliness, since Winnie and Danny were often very busy and I was often alone in London. But that was a *comfortable* loneliness, while this spot in this house that was constantly roughed about by the wind seemed perhaps the loneliest spot in the whole world. Most British children probably think that living in a tower at the top of a house by the sea would be a wonderful thing. Perhaps they might think it "educational," as Winnie would say. Or "quite amusing," as Danny would add. But I couldn't get away from that wind or the sea or the sound of the sea. At night, the moon seemed to be following me and pestering me as I turned in my bed, and it was a big, yellow, noisy American moon.

It actually happened on the third night, when I was getting up to go to the loo. (The Bathburns called it a bathroom.) I hadn't gone halfway down the stairs in the darkness, when a shadowy someone came from the front of the house and passed along the corridor and stood near that locked door not far from the door I was to steer clear of. I heard the sound of a key clicking and turning. I heard a door open and then shut. Then I heard the door being locked from the inside.

I came down the stairs ever so quietly. I inched along the hall, breathing slowly in, slowly out, though I suppose I should have been minding my manners, as Winnie would say. I passed the door I was to stay away from. It was silent and dark. But there was a light coming from under the other door. Someone was shuffling papers about in there.

I waited for a while afraid to move, but no one came out, and my feet were very cold. I had chilblains on my toes from our British winters and that meant that when my toes got even a little bit cold, they became terribly itchy. I was feeling itchy, itchy, itchy all over. And so I hurried back up to my bed, lightly running, barely touching the floor with my feet. But I lay there all night hearing the ocean howling and the wind whining, all the while listening for the click of a door key and wondering why that room was locked in the first place.

I had been trying all night to think of a way to get back to my Winnie and Danny. I wanted a plan, a way out of here. Where was my passport or my ticket home? My mum, Winnie, was British, but my dad, Danny, was all-American, so that meant I could have what Uncle Gideon called "dual citizenship," which he thought was so super, but I thought it was miserable. Most British children like to feel they belong and I did not belong here, especially tonight after hearing those slow footsteps shuffling down the hall.

★ Five ★

In the morning, it was still raining. They were saying in the newspaper that this was the wettest spring they'd had in Bottlebay for many years. In the daylight, none of the Bathburns mentioned anything about anyone unlocking doors in the middle of the night. There was no mention of trays of food that went up and came down untouched. But when I looked through the stairwell from my room, I saw The Gram hugging Auntie Miami in the hallway, and Auntie seemed to be crying. "Time will come, dear," The Gram was saying to her. "Time will come." Then they started whispering and I thought I heard my new nickname, Flissy. They went on down to the kitchen, and soon I could hear pans crashing about and I could smell more of those muffins cooking.

There was a wooden-paneled room at the end of the hall upstairs, a kind of little gymnasium. As I came downstairs, I could see Uncle Gideon in there. I sort of leaned out of sight and put my ear against the door that I was supposed to stay away from. I was quite sure by now that if there *was* a Captain Derek, this would have to be his room. I also felt quite certain that it was Uncle Gideon sneaking about last night, unless it was Captain Derek.

"Good morning, Flissy," said Uncle Gideon, who was now standing on his head in the gymnasium. "I've had breakfast and I'm already on my head. I've always been able to stand on my head, and my brother Danny never could get the hang of it. What do you think? Am I doing all right? Have you ever seen Danny do this? I bet not. How am I doing?"

"Speaking of my Danny," I said, "would you mind saying when they are coming back? How many days does 'soon' usually mean?" I was very sober and stared straight at him.

"Oh, well, um, yes, we could talk about that later. But, um, could you do me a favor in the meantime and look out the window up front and see if our mailman is coming down the beach with our mail?" he said. His face had turned very red. Then he fell over, crashing down on the floor in a very awkward way. Soon he sat up looking a bit dazed. "Danny can't do that," he said softly. "I suppose you will be having breakfast now, but we can talk about it at lunch. Do you call it lunch in Britain or is that your tea?"

"Tea is our supper," I said.

"Oh, super," said Uncle Gideon. "I've got that straight, I think."

I looked out the window down to the beach below. "Oh, there's the postman," I said, hopping up and down, first on one foot and then on the other so as not to play favorites.

"Well, then run and get the mail for us, will you, Fliss?" Uncle Gideon said, getting out of answering my question altogether, I thought. It was rather obvious.

At the front door, I stuffed my feet into my tall, black rubber Wellington boots, which we call wellies in England, and I threw myself down the many wooden steps in the rain to the beach and the sea below. Mr. Henley was the postman, and I thought he was terrifically polite and cheerful. I was ever so pleased to be rushing back to the house with a newspaper and a postcard for The Gram from someone named Jane in Chicago. But The Gram and my uncle were standing in the shadowy hall, watching me again.

"This was probably not a good idea," said Uncle Gideon, frowning at me.

"Oh, I don't see it could do any harm. She can just leave the letters on the dining room table," said The

Gram. "You wouldn't open a letter, Flissy, if it wasn't addressed to you, would you?"

I shook my head no.

Now I was quite sure I wanted to go home. For a moment, it felt like I had a crying box stuck in my throat, like the one Wink had in his stomach. If you poked Wink there, he used to make a crying noise, but his crying box was broken now. You could poke away these days, and Wink was always silent.

Uncle Gideon patted me on the top of my head again, but his hand was rough and awkward like a great bear's paw, and one of my braids got caught on his cuff link. "Okay, then, Fliss?" he said. "Okay? Fine?"

I went off into the parlor without exactly answering him. I was listening instead to a lovely song in my head that reminded me of England. I stood by the velvet curtains, halfway humming and standing on one foot. Aunt Miami was in there. She was all dressed up in a purple taffeta dress with a rose pinned in her hair. Aunt Miami was reading *Romeo and Juliet* again.

After a while, even though I was switching from one foot to the other, both feet were getting ever so tired. Auntie nodded at me and patted the cushion on the sofa next to her. I finally gave up and went over and sat beside her.

She was reading aloud the scene in which one night Romeo stands in the courtyard below Juliet's bedroom. Aunt Miami read those words with great feeling.

Then Uncle Gideon came barging in, saying, "See what I mean about being stuck, Flissy? She just keeps reading *Romeo and Juliet* over and over again. There are other wonderful books in the world. What do you say, Fliss? Do you agree? Isn't it so?"

Aunt Miami sighed and held the book up, covering her face.

"Alas," said Uncle Gideon, "we Bathburns are a lonely lot. All we know is the wind. None of us have gotten mixed up with life. Your aunt Miami is a frustrated actress. She wants the stage! She wants lights! Applause! But does she do anything about it? No. Typical Bathburn."

"What about my dad, Danny?" I said. "He's a Bathburn."

Uncle Gideon didn't answer. He looked down at his feet instead and then he looked away altogether.

Aunt Miami said, "Oh, Danny's different. He's the daring, brilliant one. It's always been like that."

"I see," I said to myself.

"Anyway, you mustn't listen to *him*," Miami said, pointing to Uncle Gideon. "He's a big tease and doesn't know beans. If you hang around with him, by the time your parents get back you will be completely confused."

By the time my parents get back. That's what Auntie Miami said. It was lovely to hear those words.

Dear Winnie and Danny,

I was outside today even though it was still raining. I made huge letters out of sand, ones that you can read from high up. The letters said "I Love You, Winnie and Danny" stretched across the beach, so if you happen to fly over in an airplane, look down and see it.

Love,

Fliss

P.S. That's what Uncle Gideon calls me. I can't get used to it at all. Miami says Gideon thinks he's hot potatoes cause he's got the same name as the Gideon Bible.

★ *Six* ★

The smokestacks were painted gray; in fact, the whole enormous ship was painted gray; even the windows were painted out, covered in gray and sealed shut. That was how I came to America, on the HMS *Queen Anne*'s maiden voyage and it had to be secret because the waters were full of German U-boats. They had to sneak the *Queen Anne* over the ocean to New York City. The windows were painted over so no light would escape, so no bomber at night, flying overhead, could spot the *Queen Anne* sailing along in great silence. Winnie and Danny and I were some of the few passengers on that boat. It had been built to be a luxury liner, but it was now being moved to an American harbor for safekeeping.

And the whole enormous dark boat was empty except for us and a handful of other passengers and a small crew. There were long empty dining rooms, tilting dark corridors, vacant lonely staterooms with their portholes painted over.

We got on the boat at night. Danny had talked to an officer friend for a long time, trying to convince him to let us board. "We are American citizens and we need to go home," he said. We waited in the small dimly lit office with some other people. We hadn't been able to find any boat that would take us to America. We heard about another British boat, the SS *Athenia*, that had been full of Americans going home and had been sunk by a German U-boat.

But Winnie and Danny were not scared. They played cards all night in that office, waiting to hear. I slept on my suitcases with my head on my stuffed bear, Wink. Danny said later it was Wink that turned the tide. The officer finally just couldn't say no.

When I stood on the huge pier on the second level that cold night and looked at the enormous *Queen Anne* all dressed in her gray war costume, I thought I might faint. I had never seen anything so big in all my life. We boarded quietly and quickly and lay in our tiny room belowdecks listening to the churning engine carrying us through dangerous waters to America.

Everything on the boat was bolted down, all the chairs, all the many tables in the dining room, a sea of tables, and we were only a tiny group of people sitting in a corner being quiet, listening for a U-boat or a torpedo, listening overhead for a bomber. For the whole eight days, we never saw the sky. And there was a storm at sea and we heard that the waves were as steep as mountains rising gray, higher than we could imagine. Winnie was sick in the hall, and I found a room with a huge swimming pool with no water in it, and the stairs were wide and empty, and most of the time we didn't speak and when we did, all our voices echoed.

★ *Seven* ★

In June, the sky continued to drizzle and drip in Bottlebay, Maine, USA, and I wrote a letter every day to Winnie and Danny. Most of the time, I tried not to talk to anyone except for Wink. He was quite playful really when we were alone, but with the Bathburns, he too fell silent. The Gram went into town for supplies a couple of times and I was invited along, but I always looked up at the sky instead of answering. Finally, one day I said, "Oh, all right. I'll go," but only because I *had* to.

And that very morning at the end of June, it stopped raining. It stopped and it stopped and it stopped. And the sun did come out and the sky was a hot summer blue and a few people appeared on the beach below with sun umbrellas and pails and towels.

If you are feeling uneasy, sometimes a blue sky can make things worse. Better to have the sky match how you feel than to have it be so lovely out while you are so dark and rainy and lonely inside.

"Riding into town with The Gram, eh? Taking your life in your hands, are you?" said Uncle Gideon, slapping the side of the old black automobile that he had just backed out of the barn for us.

I frowned to keep the sun out of my eyes and waited while Uncle Gideon helped The Gram ever so gently into the car. She smiled up at him from the driver's seat with her white hair slipping slowly out of its bun in the wind. I hadn't seen The Gram smile much before. Then I heard Uncle Gideon say very quietly, "I do think this is a good idea. We *should* introduce her to the town. Better not to raise any suspicions about *anything*."

"Well, Flissy, perhaps you'd like to buy some supplies to make a proper British tea for us," said The Gram quite loudly, shaking her head at Uncle Gideon.

"Jolly good, old thing," said Uncle Gideon. "Isn't that what they say over there? 'Old thing'? I'd love to have a real British cup of tea again."

"Have you had one before?" I said, feeling the word *suspicion* floating round now in my head.

"But, of course, Flissy," said Uncle Gideon, "I'm very fond of England." And he put his hand over his heart and looked at me in a mournful sort of way. "I certainly know the difference between a good cup of tea and a bad one. And I went to university there, you know."

"Oh," I said.

We were standing in the scruffy grass, looking at the Packard, which was ever so much bigger than our little Austin Minor in England. All the British cars were so much smaller. We were standing there in the bright morning sun, with wild rosebushes all round us being bumped and battered about in the wind.

"Well, Fliss, the windows are all broken, so don't try to roll them up and down. And The Gram doesn't like to go in reverse, so don't get yourself in any situations where you have to back up. And don't try to open the door on the passenger side. It's jammed. But otherwise, have a good time!"

"Gideon dear, we don't need any more instructions. Stand aside. Now get in, Flissy McBee." The Gram started the motor with great pizzazz, as Uncle Gideon would say, like she was just settling into a Halifax bomber and getting ready to take off.

"Be careful, Mother," said Gideon, backing away, frowning, and then waving. He stood there waving and waving and waving.

We drove out onto the road. It was a hot morning and we wound our way along the sea through the gnarled and knotted low-growing bushes and little rocky patches.

And suddenly I remembered being on holiday once with Winnie and Danny. We had a motorcycle with a dear little green sidecar. Danny was driving the motorcycle (Winnie always said he was a bit wild), and Winnie and I were snuggled into the sidecar. We were whizzing past the chalk downs and the chalk cliffs along the sea in Sussex and we could see the white cliffs of Dover in the distance. Danny stopped the motorcycle and we climbed a great grassy hill to see the Long Man of Wilmington, which was a fig-ure, a great white chalk outline of a man carved on the side of the hill hundreds of years ago. Danny said it was something only someone from high up in the sky could really clearly see all at once, like a God or an angel or an airplane pilot. I wondered about the German bombers flying over England on their way to London. I wondered if they saw the Long Man of Wilmington on a hill in the green grass not far from the ocean.

The Gram was looking over at me. "You're very pensive, Flissy," she said. Then she beeped the horn for no reason at all and said, "What a horn! They just don't make them like this anymore!" Then she looked over at me again. "Flissy, don't worry about any ques-tions people might ask you today. Just say 'la-de-da' to all of them."

I nodded.

She smiled and beeped the horn again and then she looked over at me in a worried sort of way.

Finally, we took a turn on the road that headed away from the ocean into town. "Now, keep your eyes out for a nice parker where I won't need to back up to get out," said The Gram. "And we'll just do our marketing and we won't meander at all. We won't get mixed up with those ladies at the church with their quilt sale today."

But the only "parker" that The Gram and I could find in all of Bottlebay, Maine, was right in front of the white wooden church with a tall, white wooden tower where the quilt sale was going on. A sign said, QUILT SALE, RAISING MONEY FOR THE BRITISH WAR EFFORT. No sooner had The Gram and I climbed out of the Packard through the only working door on the driver's side, when one of the women from the sale, wearing an apron, hurried towards us.

"Hello. Hello. Hello, Helen Bathburn! Where have you been keeping yourself? This just isn't like you. Come on over to our sale," she said. "You should have put in one of *your* quilts. And who is this, may I ask?"

"This is my granddaughter, Flissy McBee," said The Gram, pulling me tightly against her.

"A granddaughter? And you didn't tell us? Which of your children is married?"

"Oh, Danny was married some years ago while he was away in England," said The Gram.

"Oh, really? It wasn't in the papers. It's as if Danny disappeared into thin air. And Gideon doesn't ever have a good word to say about him anymore. It's such a shame. Well, if Danny's home, we'd love to come out and see him. It was so daring the way he once saved Marge Peterson when she was drowning."

"Well, actually he's not here right now," said The Gram, putting her hand up to shield her eyes suddenly as if she was feeling ill.

"Oh. Where is he, still overseas? Doing what?"

"Well, Danny is in sales now. You know how charming he is. He could sell salt water to the sea!" The Gram said. Everybody laughed. The Gram swallowed and started rapidly nodding at several people on the other side of the lawn. Then someone else came up to her, and The Gram was hurried away, leaving me to stare at the quilts draped on lines between the trees. I wasn't sure what my Danny did for work, but I didn't think he was in sales. I looked among the hanging quilts. Walking through the sunlight and the shadows the quilts cast, I suddenly felt lost, as if I were in a maze.

I hurried towards a table at the front of the church, where someone was in charge of the money.

"We're having a raffle today," a lady said. "It only costs ten cents. Have you got ten cents? Just write out someone's name and phone number and put it in the box. And you could win something if your ticket gets drawn."

"What do you win?" I asked.

"Oh, all sorts of things. There's a list of the prizes on the sheet over there. Are you British? You'll be helping Mr. Churchill with his war if you put a name in." She pushed a piece of paper at me and smiled.

"I am very fond of Mr. Churchill. He's our lovely prime minister in England," I said.

British children are usually ever so polite, and they always obey adults whenever they can. If an adult tells a British child to put a name in for a raffle, they do it. And so I did. I paid ten cents for Mr. Churchill and I wrote a name and a telephone number on the piece of paper. I stuffed it in the box, not realizing then how such a small act might one day come round to haunt me.

Soon enough, The Gram was back and the other woman was handing me a flyer. "We're doing a variety show this fall at the town hall. Could you pin this up in the grocery for us, dear?"

After that, we didn't meander about at all. We walked down a shady street and turned a corner, and there were all the shops in Bottlebay, Maine. We got right down to shopping. The Gram let me pick out a tin of Earl Grey and some cold cuts for my proper British tea. I fancied a box of biscuits, but The Gram waved at the air and said, "No, no, Flissy. We make all our cookies out at the house."

She bought the groceries while I went over to pin up the flyer on the bulletin board. As we left the store, The Gram seemed to be in a shall-we-get-out-of-here sort of mood, as if she didn't want to answer any more questions.

It was on the way home in the windy car that I began to think things over. Why had The Gram told her friends that Danny worked as a salesman? And why did she seem to avoid talking about him? And what about the sea captain? Why didn't he come out of his room, anyway? Was someone even in there? I mean actually, really, truly?

Once we got out of town, The Gram kept looking over at me again and beeping the horn and saying, "Well, we made it, Flissy McBee. We'll soon be home."

The ride was bumpy and the sky darkening. I tried not to, but I fell asleep as we drove along. When we finally pulled into the driveway, I awoke and found a blanket covering me, and lying in my lap was a little sack. I looked in it and there was the box of biscuits I had fancied at the store.

By now, it was dusk and as we climbed out of the car, the house was all dark. The moon hung out over the ocean, and clouds of mist and spray floated in the black air.

"Where are the electric lights?" said The Gram. "You know we only had those installed recently. I hope they haven't shorted out in the wind. Hello! Miami, are you there?"

We went in the back door, and The Gram turned on the kitchen light and set the grocery bag on the blue metal table. I went on down the dark hall, hearing music coming from the front parlor. A sad record was playing. The parlor was completely dark. I stopped at the entrance and listened.

When the clouds roll by
and the moon drifts through
When the haze is high
I think of you.
I think of you.

When the mist is sheer
and the shadows too

When the moon is spare
I think of you.
I think of you.

My eyes slowly adjusted to the darkness and I could see someone sitting in the armchair in the corner, someone lost in the music. Then the hall light was turned on behind me, and I could see instantly it was Uncle Gideon sitting in there alone.

"Fliss?" he said. "Oh, I thought everyone had gone to town. Um, well, I'm just listening to a record, just, you know. This song is, um, a Bathburn favorite. Actually, the record belongs to Derek, but, well..."

"Sorry," I said, "I didn't mean to interrupt."

"No, no, no, Fliss, it's fine. You're fine. It's always nice to see you. Really."

"The record belongs to Captain Derek, then?" I said.

"Yes, he collects records, you know."

"Oh, well, then, Captain Derek *really* is here?"

"Oh, yes," said Uncle Gideon. "Of course he is. And hopefully he'll be down soon. Time will tell, Flissy. Time will tell."

The sweet, sad song played on, and Uncle Gideon grew quiet then and seemed to become lost again in his own thoughts.

Eight

The postman was early that morning and I ran barefoot down the long wooden steps to the beach. The postman always walked up the shoreline instead of along the road above. He had his postman's cap off and his hair was all breezy. "He's young, that one," The Gram had said to me earlier. "That's why he takes the long way around, because it's more fun and he hasn't yet learned not to waste time. Like you, Flissy, when you walk in circles to cross a room when a straight line would get you there faster."

Today, the postman was pleased because all week he'd had nothing but rubbish for us and now he had some *real* mail. It makes postmen feel miserable and foolish when you come running towards them and all they have to give you is an unpleasant looking electric bill. But today he looked all chipper and important and he held out a letter. The envelope was covered with brightly colored stamps, and in the corner was a little blue rectangle with the words By Airplane and Par Avion. Those are the sorts of letters that usually come across the ocean.

The letter was addressed to Gideon Bathburn. I looked for a postmark and I thought it said something like *Portugal.* One side of the envelope was stamped with a triangle that said Passed by censor #82.

"Thank you, Mr. Henley," I said in my best British English. "Thank you ever so much." And then I tore up the steps.

Uncle Gideon seemed suddenly to be at the top of the stairs on the porch. I thought he tried to appear awfully casual, whistling and swinging his arms back and forth. I looked down at the letter again and recognized my Danny's handwriting. His *H*s and *R*s always looked like little waving people. I held on to the letter tightly. "This is from Danny!" I said when I got to the top of the stairs. I couldn't stop jumping up and down. "It's from Danny!!!!"

"No, it's not," said Uncle Gideon. "Give it to me now, and don't go off with my mail, Flissy. Ever."

"Let me see it," I said.

"No," he said loudly, grabbing the letter in a brusque way. He tucked it into his pocket. Then he turned immediately towards the house. But soon he stopped and looked back and said, "Flissy, perhaps we can play Parcheesi later. What do you say?"

"No," I said. "I want to see the letter from my father."

A terrible look of pain came over Uncle Gideon's face. He turned round abruptly and went into the house, the screen door snapping shut behind him with a loud, flat slap. I heard him climb the long stairs, walk down the hall up there, pause for a moment, and then he unlocked the locked door quietly and stepped in, closing the door behind him.

I thought so, I said to myself. I knew it was my uncle Gideon who had been stealing about in the middle of the night, turning locks and closing doors.

Really, I felt very sorry indeed for my curiosity. Winnie always said that my curiosity was my best feature and also my worst feature. But Danny used to make his *H*s and *R*s into little drawings of people on paper for me, people who talked and made alphabet jokes. Because I knew his *H*s and his *R*s, all sorts of questions started piling up inside me, the way seashells and sea glass and pieces of driftwood pile up along the beach after a storm. Why couldn't I see a letter from my Danny? Why was it from Portugal, instead of from England? No one here exactly answered *any* of my questions. So I got out my knitting, my wool and my needles, and I started in.

British children, well, girls really, knit all the time. If you were ever to ride an English omnibus, you would look about and see all the girls and women knitting. Danny always said, "I've never seen a British baby knitting yet, but it wouldn't surprise me."

Today, I was knitting a pair of red socks for Wink. Poor, poor Wink. He hated Bottlebay, Maine. And he had a terrible thing happen to him. Before we left London, someone slit him open along his seam in front and put a small object inside him and sewed him back up before Danny and Winnie and I got on the boat. I could feel the little object in there next to his crying box when I hugged Wink. But then by the time we got to Maine, the metal object was gone, and Wink was all sewed up right again.

Nine

Aunt Miami and Uncle Gideon often played Parcheesi in the darkened parlor in the morning. The next day, they sat at a table in the curtained bay window. As I stood in the hallway just outside the room, Uncle Gideon was saying, "Oh, come on, Miami, give up. I've got you now."

"You've cheated, again," said Aunt Miami, "and I want a rematch."

"Whining and pining will get you nowhere," he said.

"*You* should talk," she said. "You're the one who lives in the past."

"Won't you come and have a go at Parcheesi, Flissy? Isn't that what they say in jolly old England? 'Have a go'? We'll start afresh. You might very well like it, even though I *am* the undisputed champion," said Uncle Gideon, wiggling his eyebrows up and down, trying to be funny. I hadn't realized he even knew I was standing in the hall.

Miami threw some cards from another game in his face and they fluttered about and fell all over him. He looked very docile sitting there with cards on his shoulders and cards in his lap. But he didn't fool me.

"Fliss, we need you. Parcheesi with three is much more of a challenge. Please?" he said.

"Probably no," I said, going into the room and flopping down on the sofa. "I'm quite busy, actually."

"Extremely urgent, is it?" he said, smiling.

"Oh, all right," I said. "But it's too dark in here to see the game board clearly." I stood up and went over to the curtains. I saw the curtain cord hanging there along the window and I pulled it and the curtains went swishing off and away from the many windows. The room was suddenly filled with morning sunlight.

Uncle Gideon looked at me quickly. Then he stared down at his hands. Finally, he said quietly, "Lovely, Fliss. Perfect. Pull up a chair."

"Beware," said Miami, whispering to me, "he sneaks around and seems to know everything and he *always* wins."

★ ☆ ★

"Oh, come now, it's only a game, you two," Uncle Gideon said later, after he had crushed us both at Parcheesi and we were sitting there feeling like two smashed-up fishing boats side by side on the beach. Uncle Gideon looked over at us in a terribly cheerful way.

Then Auntie got out a photo album and we saw pictures of Danny when he was eleven years old, the day he climbed the huge boat launch in the harbor and hung upside down by his knees over the water, smiling at the camera. In all the photographs, my Danny always seemed to be in the center, beaming in his handsome way, and Uncle Gideon always seemed to be lost in the background.

I was just going to ask again about Danny's letter when The Gram poked her head through the parlor door. "That son of mine. That Danny Bathburn. It's a wonder you are such a sensible girl, Flissy, when your father, Danny, never showed any sense at all right from the start." She sighed and closed her eyes and then she went over and hugged Aunt Miami. She seemed to hold on to her terribly tightly because her thin, small hands turned white and tense against Miami's lavender sweater.

"My Danny is very clever, and so is Winnie," I said in a loud way.

"Yes," Uncle Gideon said. He looked quite dismal for a moment. Then he suddenly announced that he wanted to make me a little bed for Wink and would I fetch Wink for measurements. "Now that you are eleven, Fliss, don't you think Wink ought to have his own sleeping quarters? Wouldn't that be a step in the right direction? You should give him his independence," said Uncle Gideon, smiling at me again.

I had to admit he did sometimes have a nice smile. It had a sort of bearish warmth to it, reminding me ever so slightly of Wink when Wink was thinking about something fondly. But then hadn't Uncle Gideon just beaten Auntie and me at Parcheesi, showing no mercy at all and being terribly gleeful about it? And why was he so gruff about Danny's letter?

I frowned and didn't exactly answer him. I just left the room on my way to get Wink. I was stomping up the stairs, feeling grumpy and puzzled by everything. If I still depended on Wink, it wasn't my fault. My teacher in London had said it was Winnie's fault. Winnie had cried then and said her work was "very pressing." I had been ever so embarrassed.

I was just running past what I had guessed was Derek's door. But then, I stopped. I *heard* something. It was music, jazzy mournful music coming from in there. Captain Derek collected records. He liked jazz, I was told. How strange that I hadn't met him. How strange that he hadn't come out and that I hadn't even *seen* him at all.

I forgot all about losing dreadfully at Parcheesi. I sat down on the hall floor and listened to the music. I leaned my head back and imagined for a moment that I was ice-skating with Winnie and Danny. I loved skating with them on a pond in Hampstead Heath, but we only went once. They never had time to go again.

I sat back up and looked at Captain Derek's door. Right then and there, I made up my mind. I went upstairs to write Captain Derek a note.

Dear Captain Derek,

My name is Felicity Bathburn Budwig AKA Flissy. I am Danny Bathburn's little girl. Have you ever played Parcheesi with Uncle Gideon? Do you think he cheats? Auntie thinks so. I thought the music was lovely. I should be very pleased to meet you. Will you be coming downstairs any time soon?

Yours most sincerely,

Felicity Bathburn Budwig

I daresay British children don't usually do rash and daring things without asking an adult first, but then I do have a bit of Danny in me and perhaps that part was to blame. Anyway, I took that note and on my way back downstairs, I shoved it under Captain Derek's door. Then I took Wink into the parlor, and he got fitted for a brand-new bed. Uncle Gideon drew me a picture of the way the bed would look when it was finished. It was lovely, and I said, "It's jolly nice, Uncle Gideon. I'm not half chuffed."

"Not half chuffed? Now what is that?" he said.

"*Not half chuffed* means 'pleased.' I'm very pleased," I said.

"I see," said Uncle Gideon, and after that, he used *not half chuffed* over and over again, every chance he got, all the while smiling at me.

Then, while The Gram had her back turned, Uncle Gideon popped into the kitchen and swiped a cookie from the just-for-Sunday cookie jar. And he tried to look all sweet and sheepish so I wouldn't tell. Anyway, British children are not snitches. So he got away with it. (Besides, he ended up sneaking one out for me.)

After supper, I went into the library. "Well, who is that letter from, then, if it's not from my Danny?" I said, crossing my arms and standing there very solemnly.

Uncle Gideon looked over the top of his reading glasses at me and said, "Just from an old school buddy of mine, that's all, Fliss."

But I didn't believe him.

"By the way, have you read anything decent lately?" he said. And he handed me a book called *A Little Princess* by Frances Hodgson Burnett. A British writer.

I said thank you and took the book, but I still didn't believe him. I curled up in a chair and studied the cover of the book and wondered what it would feel like to have a middle name like Hodgson.

In my bed that night with poor Wink, I thought about that letter from Portugal with the colorful foreign stamps all over it and Danny's adorable *H*s and I was ever, ever so sorry, but I knew I had to read it. I just *had* to know, only because I missed Winnie and Danny so much. I sat up in my bed and watched the ocean in the dark and I could see the lights of a tanker going across the horizon in the distance and I wondered if that tanker was going all the way to England.

★ Ten ★

Before you knew it, I was ever so regretful that I had pushed the letter to Captain Derek *all* the way under the door. Because if I had pushed it *halfway* under, then I would have known if someone had pulled it through and picked it up. Now, for all I knew, the letter I wrote might have been lying there in the shadows unread, unnoticed. It was for that reason that I wrote another letter.

> *Dear Captain Derek,*
>
> *It's me again, the one they call Flissy Bathburn. Sorry to bother you. But some things have been happening out here in your absence that perhaps you may be interested in. First of all, Uncle Gideon has received a letter from Portugal, and he has acted very strangely about it and quite frankly lied (in my opinion). I am very curious now and worried. Do you think he is hiding something concerning my parents? I hope you got one of my biscuits. I made them with The Gram. When*

you come out, you can meet Wink. He is very
shy too.

    Yours,
    Felicity Bathburn Budwig

This time I was very much more clever. I tucked the letter halfway under the door and I waited. Even though I could hear Uncle Gideon calling, "Fliss dear, could you come down here and take a little walk on the beach with your aunt Miami? She's just gotten to the poison part of *Romeo and Juliet* and she's all gloomy and talking about never getting to play Juliet, that it's too late for her and the stage and all that."

And Aunt Miami called back, "Oh, don't listen to him, Flissy. *He's* the one who's letting his talent go to waste."

I barely heard them. I was watching that letter halfway under the door. And then, just as I was about to turn round and go downstairs, the letter moved. Someone pulled it under the door.

My heart started racing and thumping and spinning, carrying on inside me like a tiny sparrow in a new cage. I was scared and nervous and pleased all at once. It was a jolly nice feeling to realize that I had run a test and it had worked. I had proved that Captain Derek existed.

He *was* in there. It made me think that I *can* be a clever girl, even though I can't do long division.

"Flissy, you're all fidgety again," said The Gram when I came downstairs with my hand strangely over my face, trying to hide what I had just discovered. "I think a nice long walk will be a good thing. Take your time, now."

Auntie shrugged and patted me on the back. "Come along, Flissy Miss," she said. "Are you up for a stroll?"

The Gram handed us a packed lunch. Then she whispered something in Auntie's ear. And everything seemed to turn dark again and that feeling came over me, that feeling of being a little boat cast out to sea with no flag to raise on the deck and no port to turn to.

We clumped down the long steps to the beach. Then we edged along the water silently because Auntie was often quiet. The tide was out, so we could walk on the hard sand that is usually under the ocean, and we saw all sorts of creatures lugging their homes on their backs and others lurking in tide pools, waving their claws about, looking for a good fight. I kept picking up sand dollars and putting them in my dress pocket, wishing they were called "sand shillings" instead. In England, everyone thought Americans called dollars "bucks." We thought everyone lived on cattle ranches and said, "I've got ten

bucks that says that cowpoke won't make it to Wyoming."
But so far, I hadn't heard the Bathburns say anything
like that.

Without talking at all, Aunt Miami and I walked
way out to the end of the jetty. Then Auntie stood on the
very tip of the point, swaying her arms in the wind.

"What a perfect place at the edge of the world to say
some poetic lines," she called out. "Do you mind?"

"No, it would be lovely," I called back. And so I sat
down on a rock, with the tide slowly rolling in. Auntie
turned in circles, and the wind rippled and ruffled her
skirt, and her hair blew about. She stared up at the sky
and began,

"O Romeo, Romeo, wherefore art thou Romeo?
Deny thy father and refuse thy name…"

She went on for a while and I even joined in.

Then the sky got dark and it looked like a storm was
rolling up behind the clouds. The wind was ripping
Auntie's words apart and sending Juliet's speech flying
off into the roar.

"Auntie," I called, "I think we should go back! You
can say the rest of your speech as we run."

Auntie took my hand and we did run all the way back

from the end of the jetty to the beach. The lighthouse was sending its rolling light round and round on the choppy water. And there was a bell tolling, riding the water in a buoy off the coast to warn boats. We ran and ran and ran. The wind and rain on the sand were frightfully nasty. The sand came up and hit my arms like thousands of tiny needles, and I had to cover my eyes. We dropped our packed lunch somewhere and Auntie Miami lost one of her shoes and all the shells fell out of my pocket. Even with the wind swallowing us up, Auntie seemed hesitant as we got closer to the house.

"Come on, Auntie," I called. "Let's hurry." But she held back, looking up at the Bathburn house high above us on the ridge. The porch swing was knocking about all by itself, and one of the wicker chairs had blown off onto the ledge above us. I looked at the ocean. The waves were swelling higher and higher. Still, Auntie seemed to pull back and turn away. "Please, Auntie," I called again. "Let's go in."

Finally, I was ever so glad to grab the wooden railing of the stairs. I dragged myself up each step, though I thought the wind would toss me away like a wicker chair onto the rocks at any moment. When we got in the door, I had sand in my hair and all in my wet clothes. And there were pools of water under my feet in the hallway.

We got back much sooner than expected. The house was very quiet. And it was ever so dark. The Gram came downstairs, looking worried and tired. "Miami, it would have been better if you'd stayed out longer, dear," she said. Then Uncle Gideon came downstairs, followed by a man with a black doctor's bag. The air smelled of medicine.

Things came to me in pieces then, like a mismatching cardboard puzzle, shadowy and broken up with light and muffled noise. Was he a doctor? He must have come out of Captain Derek's room. Was Captain Derek sick, then? Is that why he stayed in there?

The Gram and the doctor and Uncle Gideon all walked past me as if I weren't there at all. They went into the parlor, closing the double doors behind them. Then I heard murmuring and mumbling and whispering. I went up close to the door, listening, but I could not make out a single word they said.

★ Eleven ★

I went into the library the next afternoon, feeling ever so sorry about Captain Derek. I hadn't even met him, and now, since he might be desperately ill, perhaps I never would. I was poking about among the shelves in the library, hoping to find a book on stamps, one with pictures in it showing what stamps exactly came from Portugal.

Suddenly, I stopped short. I noticed for the first time that under piles of newspapers and magazines in the far corner was a piano, one of those great black shiny ones shaped like the continent of South America on three legs. I went over to it and I saw that the lid of the piano, the part that covered the keys, was nailed shut with great big nails driven into the wood. I'd never seen a piano nailed shut before. I was just reaching out to feel the lid and the places where the nails had gashed and scarred the wood when, suddenly, Uncle Gideon stood up. He had been sitting deep behind a pile of books and I hadn't seen him. "Please!" he shouted out, "Please stay away from that piano. Don't touch it and don't go over there again."

I backed away towards the door.

"Oh, I am sorry, Fliss," he called after me. "I didn't mean to bark. I don't bark usually. You must know that by now. I was just angry for a moment. I was caught off guard. It's not you," he said. "I'm not angry at *you*."

I hurried out of the room and ran down the hall to the dining room. I found a big, high-backed stuffed chair and I turned it round to face the wall. I sat staring at the wallpaper.

"Flissy?" Aunt Miami said. "Are you there?"

I hadn't realized she was also sitting in the room in another high-backed chair. I never knew what to expect in this house. I very much wanted to go home. Now more than ever. So I didn't answer her. I turned my head away, tracing the tangled vines on the wallpaper. All the vines were covered with thorns, and the roses seemed squeezed and confused among the leaves.

Miami kept saying, "Flissy, are you okay?"

Finally, I said, "I was only looking at something in the library, but it bothered Uncle Gideon."

"Ah," said Miami, "the piano."

"Yes," I said. "Why is it nailed shut? Why was he so angry?"

"Oh, Flissy," said Miami, "you are too young. You wouldn't understand."

"I *would* understand," I said, standing up and stomping about.

"You would?"

"Yes," I said. "Truly."

"Well, my brother Gideon is a wonderful pianist. He can play anything and everything. But he doesn't want to play the piano anymore. So he nailed it shut."

"Why?" I said.

Miami shook her head. She leaned over and tugged on my braids twice. She touched the end of my nose three times. Then she simply got up and left the room.

★ Twelve ★

Most eleven-year-old girls are terribly posh and in England some of them even go round to parties and dance with lovely boys from Eton. My chum Lily Jones knew an eleven-year-old girl who wore lipstick in secret and had her toenails painted fire engine red. I wanted to be one of those girls; that's what I told Wink. But Wink wasn't listening. He was crying instead because there were so many secrets here, and everything seemed so odd, making him feel like a bear without a country. He felt he didn't belong anywhere. I rocked him in my arms and I said, "There, there, Wink, don't cry," and soon I was crying too, because Wink's tears always went straight to my heart.

I was not sure about anything anymore. As summer drew on, I was not sure what would happen in September with my education. Normally, in England, most eleven-year-olds had taken the Eleven Plus Test. If you failed, you had to go to Secondary Modern and learn how to be an automobile mechanic or something like that. But my school had closed because of the war and so no one had taken the test. Most children had been sent to the country to be away from the bombing anyway. I was one of the last ones to leave, except for my chum Lily Jones and her little brother, Albert. They were still in London because their mum was afraid to send them off.

I heard The Gram say earlier this morning in the hall before I got up, "Well, Miami, at least he's no longer contagious. We must be grateful for that."

Now I took a peek out my very-high-up windows and I could see the postman rounding a hill, so I took off like a bomber ripping down the stairs and flying out on the porch till The Gram called out, "Flissy B. Bathburn, where are your British manners?"

I wanted to get there before my uncle Gideon did. I wanted to see if we got another letter in an airmail envelope. Uncle Gideon was already in the ocean, having a morning swim. I could see him bobbing up and down in the cold water like a lonely seal, so I ran extra fast to get there first. The postman looked very awake this morning and handed me another letter from Portugal addressed to Uncle Gideon. Another one.

Uncle Gideon was out of the water in a flash, and most of the time he was terribly hard to get out of the water. Usually, The Gram would look out the window at Gideon in the sea and she'd say, "Bathburn is in the bathtub again." Then she would call out, "Gideon, out of the water now, dear. You're going to freeze or wrinkle up like a prune!"

Today, Uncle Gideon was already drying off. He zipped over to the postman and me. "Flissy, I'll have that. NOW!" he said, pulling the letter away from me. Then, when he had the letter firmly in his hands, he cheered up again and said, "Oh, Flissy, forgive me. But as you can see, it *is* addressed to me. Are you all right? What do you say, Fliss?"

"It's from Danny," I said again. "I know it."

"Nosy as a rule, are they, the British?" said Uncle Gideon, pretending to steal my nose, holding his thumb between his two fingers and waving it round trying to trick me.

"Not at all," I said. "Not normally."

I sat down on the last wooden step and stared out at the sea. It was calm today like a quiet mirror, like the long mirror upstairs above the marble-top chest of drawers in The Gram's room. When I had been up in that room yesterday, I had seen a framed photograph sitting there of Gideon and Danny and Miami when they were children. I had opened a top drawer, hoping to find a picture of Captain Derek, but all I found was Winnie and Danny's wedding photo stuffed way at the back. It showed them standing on a white English chalk cliff with the sea below, Winnie's bridal dress blowing about and Danny holding on to the corsage on his lapel. Both of them looked so happy. I turned the photo over and on the back it said, *"Mother, I'm sorry, you know that. I could never have imagined any of this. Miss you all. Love, Danny."*

I leaned my head against the railing, and Uncle Gideon hurried past me on the sandy steps. How was I going to read that letter? How was I going to see either letter when he always locked the door to that room? Suddenly, I wished that I wasn't a child anymore because no one ever tells children anything. Children are just supposed to guess at things, and that's very confusing because some children might guess wrong. They do in school all the time. I remember when Jillian Osgood guessed how many wellies were standing in the hall at school and she was off by two dozen.

Perhaps there would be a moment, I decided, when Uncle Gideon might forget to lock the door, just once. Just once. And then I hurried up the steps to tell Wink what I was thinking, because I didn't want Wink to feel left out and sad and full of curiosity because of unanswered, mixed-up questions.

On the way up to my room, I was just hurrying past Captain Derek's door when I spotted a folded piece of paper sticking out from under it. At first I thought I had imagined it as I ran past, and I had to stop and back up, like the Packard screeching into reverse when The Gram went down the wrong street in Bottlebay. A piece of paper? A note?

I quickly reached down and snatched it up and I couldn't wait to open it. So I did.

It said, *An answer to your questions, YES. YES. AND YES.*

★ Thirteen ★

"Flissy dear, Miami is making Romeo cookies. Would you care to help?" The Gram called from the kitchen. That kitchen in Bottlebay, Maine, was always as noisy as the sea, with pots banging and water hissing through the pipes and a teapot whistling with no one tending to it and glasses clinking and people talking. Someone was always in that kitchen poking about, making something. Once in the middle of the night, I slipped down the stairs and heard The Gram and Uncle Gideon whispering in the pantry together. Their voices sounded rapid and anxious. "Well, I'll be making a phone call to Donovan's office in the morning when everyone goes out, okay?" Uncle Gideon said. Another night, I heard him whispering to The Gram, "And what do we do about Flissy when the war is over?"

"Pop round, Fliss," called Uncle Gideon now. "Isn't that what you Brits say over there? 'Pop round.' We need an icer. Are you a good icer?"

"What's a good icer?" I said.

"Someone who's willing to put pink goop all over those silly Romeo cookies," said Uncle Gideon, rubbing his hands together.

"Oh, I'm ever so good at biscuits," I said.

"Biscuits?" said Uncle Gideon.

"Yes, they're sweet and sugary and you put them in the cooker and they come out all crisp and warm and you eat them with tea," I said.

"A cooker?" said Uncle Gideon. "A cooker is a hot day around here. We say 'Lovely day. It looks like it's going to be a cooker. Would you like a cookie?'"

"Oh, but that's silly," I said.

"Oh, well, Fliss, we'll never get things straight, will we? But we'll keep trying, won't we? Stiff upper lip and all that," said Uncle Gideon, running his finger into the pink icing. The Gram swatted his arm, and he pulled his finger out of the icing and licked it anyway.

Then he got suddenly serious and said, "Flissy, can you smile for me? You haven't smiled much. You have such a lovely smile. Do you know that?"

I turned my head away.

"She misunderstands your jokes, Gideon. He's very kindhearted," said The Gram to me, "really and truly."

Uncle Gideon just stood there with a dab of pink icing on the end of his nose, his folded hands resting on the table before him.

I tasted part of a cookie. Then I started to help Aunt Miami dribble pink, pink, ever so pink icing all over the Romeo cookies. They were all shaped like hearts. And it wasn't Saint Valentine's Day. It was a sunny day in July. And it was going to be a cooker.

The whole time I was smooshing that pink goop all over those hearts, I was thinking about Captain Derek and the note he wrote back to me. *Yes, Yes, and Yes* was all it said. But that was all it needed to say. Yes, Uncle Gideon cheated at Parcheesi. I thought so. Even though he seemed cheerful and sweet and was making Wink a new bear bed. Even though he was right about Frances Hodgson Burnett having written a ripping good story for children. And yes, Uncle Gideon was hiding something from me.

I just kept smearing pink on all the Romeo hearts, and the whole while I was thinking about Winnie and Danny. I wanted to explain to all the Bathburns how wonderful they were. I wanted to say that Winnie and Danny were so very intelligent. Winnie could embroider anything and faster than lightning and she could read a whole book in a day, while it was taking me two weeks to finish *A Little Princess*. And Winnie could speak three languages with a lovely accent. Someone came to our flat to make sure her French accent was perfect. The woman was called a coach. Danny was like that too with French, German, and Italian. They met at a posh university in England called Oxford and they studied things like that. And if I should ever talk with an American child who would say that I do not have parents at all, I would show them the photo of Winnie and Danny and me walking across the body of the Long Man of Wilmington in East Sussex County, England.

We had just finished the last Romeo heart and there wasn't enough icing and so it only covered half a heart, and Uncle Gideon made a joke about it being a half-hearted sort of Romeo, and Auntie got her revenge by taking a wooden spoon still covered in pink icing and smooshing it on Uncle's cheek and then he began to chase her with a sifter full of flour, and they ran out onto the porch and down the steps towards the sea.

The Gram rolled her eyes at me. "Can you believe that girl is thirty-two years old? You wouldn't know it, would you," she said. Then she went on preparing a tray with two teacups and a pot of tea and a plate of Romeo hearts and two napkins. Then she lifted the tray off the table and handed it to me, saying, "Flissy dear, take this up to Captain Derek, will you? And cheer him up if you can. He's been a bit sick."

★ *Fourteen* ★

Take a tea tray to Captain Derek? How could I ever do that? I'd been here a whole month and a half and I'd never laid eyes on him. I had no idea who he was at all. After all this time, I had become, well, scared and rather shy to meet him.

British children are usually very brave. I saw many, many of them getting on trains in London, saying good-bye to their mums and dads, going alone to the countryside to get away from the bombs. And yet most of them didn't cry. They kept a stiff upper lip, as Uncle Gideon would say, trying to pretend to be British. One day, Uncle Gideon had on a fake handlebar mustache and a silly riding jacket and he was horsing about in the library, teasing Auntie and me with his fake British accent, pretending he was on horseback and that he was going off hunting and all that nonsense. I did finally laugh, but only because I couldn't help it. I did hope Captain Derek was more sedate.

I set the tray down for a moment and I tucked Wink under my arm and then I picked up the tray again. I just wasn't going to go up there without Wink. So I climbed the stairs with the tea tray rattling in my arms, and with every step, I was thinking about that nice, big, fat Mr. Winston Churchill, our prime minister, who was keeping Britain strong and safe. Danny told me that he said to the British people as the war began, "People will say of the British joining the war, this was our finest hour." Or something like that. But it wasn't my finest hour just now. I was very nervous, not having ever met Captain Derek properly, and so was Wink.

I tried to imagine what a sea captain would look like as I approached the dark wooden door. I could hear jazzy, sad music as usual coming from in there and I thought I could smell medicine again and it was all a bit spooky and ever so strange.

I knocked lightly on the door. "Captain Derek?" I called out. I could only hear that song playing and the words clearly,

When the clouds roll by
and the moon drifts through
When the haze is high

I think of you.
I think of you.

When the mist is sheer
and the shadows too
When the moon is spare
I think of you.
I think of you.

"Captain Derek?" I called again. I turned the doorknob and stepped into the very dark room. The curtains were drawn across the windows. I looked at the bed and there was someone in it, but the blankets were pulled up over that someone's head. It looked like Captain Derek had died and someone had covered him up the way they do with dead bodies. Hearing the sorrowful music and looking at the bed with the body in it all covered up, I thought I might faint, even though Uncle Gideon was always saying, "Fainting is fake, no one ever really faints. They just throw themselves on the ground to get attention."

"Captain Derek," I said and I set the tray on a little table by the bed. "I brought you some tea." I forgot to mention the biscuits, but he didn't answer anyway. I was about to call out to The Gram when a foot moved under the blanket. I saw it clearly. "Captain Derek," I said, "what did you mean by 'Yes, yes, and yes'? Would you care to say?"

"No," said a voice, "not now. Please leave."

"But we've got some nice things to eat, some sweets and a pot of English tea."

"Sweets?" said the voice.

"Yes, lovely sugary things. Cookies."

"Hand me one, then," he said.

And I put a Romeo heart on the pillow and I saw some fingers snatch it down under the covers. Then I heard some munching and crunching. "I'll have another," he said.

"Come out and say hello first," I said.

There was a long pause and suddenly the covers began to roll and shudder and I began to feel all quivery and nervous, and Captain Derek sat up straight and the covers fell back and there he was, sitting up before me.

"Oh, excuse me," I said. And I closed my mouth quickly and almost bit my tongue.

There was Captain Derek and he was not an old man with a beard or even an adult at all. Captain Derek was a boy near my age, with brown hair and a kind of nice face, rather handsome, as Winnie would say.

"*You're* Captain Derek?" I said. "But you're a child like me!"

"I'm twelve," he said. "And I'm not a child."

"But why are you called a captain?" I said.

"Because I *am* a captain to them," he said, pointing to a pile of metal soldiers lying on the rug. "I don't play with them anymore *ever.* Really. I *used* to be their captain. That's all. And anyway, why are you carrying around a bear? Isn't that for little kids?"

"Oh, he's not really just a bear," I said. "He's special. He's Wink. I know it's terribly strange. But he's quite lovely and worth all the strangeness."

"Do you always have that funny way of talking?" Captain Derek said.

"Well, to me, *you* have a funny way of talking. You sound very American," I said.

"No, I don't. I sound normal. You sound different," he said.

"I suppose I am very different," I said. "I'm British and I am planning on going home soon. I don't belong here at all." I sat down on a chair next to the bed, and I let go of Wink and he fell to the floor. Poor Wink always ended up being dropped somewhere and having to make do with staring at the underneath side of a chair.

Derek leaned against the pillows in his bed and reminded me of the handsome boy in the poem "The Land of Counterpane."

When I was sick and lay a-bed
I had two pillows at my head.

"Do you always listen to music?" I asked.

"Yes, I love jazz and I love this song called 'I Think of You.' It's my favorite. Gideon likes it too. But none of that matters because I'm not going to get out of bed ever again."

"What?" I said. "Why not?"

"Because I don't want to," he said.

"Oh," I said. "Why not?"

"Because of this." He picked up his left arm and he dropped it on the tray and it rattled the teacups and knocked a Romeo cookie onto the floor. "You see this arm. It doesn't work anymore. It's paralyzed. I can't feel it at all. That's because I've had polio."

"Oh, well," I said, "you've got the other one."

"That's not the point. I can never join the army now. They'd never have me. And soon enough everyone will be joining the army. America will join the war and I want to be a part, but now I can't." Derek lay back down and covered his head with the blanket.

"Captain Derek," I called, "do come out and talk."

"No," he shouted, "go away. Turn up the music and go away."

And so I gathered up Wink and we stood there listening to that song playing over and over again and then we walked downstairs. We went out on the porch and sat down on the swing. I looked out at the gray, rumbling, anxious sea, a sea full of secrets and questions. And I pushed the swing with my feet, back and forth, back and forth, in and out of the shadows.

★ Fifteen ★

Aunt Miami and I had just picked a bouquet of wild roses and had brought them into the house. She was arranging each stem in a vase on the table. "These are so lovely, but they won't last long. They fade in an afternoon," she said in a very wistful way, glancing up at herself in the long mirror over the mantel.

"Auntie," I said, "about Derek. Why didn't anyone tell me?"

"Oh, Flissy," she said, turning round. Her eyes were not exactly blue but, rather, violet. "We didn't want to frighten you, because polio is quite contagious. We hoped Winnie and Danny would leave you here. We didn't want to give them any reason *not* to. And it's fine now. Derek is all better."

"But his arm will never be all better, and he won't come out of his room. He won't even get out of his bed," I said.

Miami went to the window and stood with her back to me.

"But why didn't Winnie and Danny tell me anything about Derek before I got here?" I said. "They didn't know there even *was* a Derek."

"Well, yes, twelve years ago, you know, there was a great rift among the Bathburns."

"What is a rift?" I said.

"A great big terrible tear in the fabric of this family," she said.

Just then, The Gram stopped at the doorway. Her face looked cloudy as if she was wearing a dark veil over her eyes. She shook her head back and forth.

"You're wandering into trouble, Miami. Come to the pantry immediately. I need some help cleaning out the icebox," she said.

After that, silence covered the room like fog, like the fog we got in the mornings here, drifting over the point. I sat down with Wink on the sofa. I had my arm round him because I knew how he was feeling. "There, there, Wink," I whispered. "There, there."

In the newspaper, I had seen photographs of people in Europe carrying suitcases, long lines of them leaving one country for another because of the war. They were called refugees and they didn't belong anywhere either. Not belonging is a terrible feeling. It feels awkward and it hurts, as if you were wearing someone else's shoes.

★ ☆ ★

It was already early July, and it was hot and windy and I spent a lot of time wading about alone in the sea. No one came to the house at all or rang up on the telephone. Sometimes, I would see Uncle Gideon taking his very long walk, but otherwise no one left the house much. The beach was empty a lot of the time because The Gram said everyone went to the other side of the point, where the ocean had bigger waves. Uncle Gideon had Wink's bed all cut out, but he hadn't had time to put it together yet, so it lay about in the library, looking like a big puzzle on the table.

The house and the Bathburns were also a puzzle to me, but at least now I had found Derek, though things had not improved with him at all. He had not put one toe out of his room or even out of his bed (except for trips to the loo), as far as I could tell. It was my job to bring up his tray of food every day. Every morning, I would set the tray down on the table across the room and say, "If you would like breakfast, Derek, it's here on the table."

He would peek out from the covers and say, "Bring it over here, please."

Then I would say, "No."

And he would say, "Yes."

And I would say, "No."

And he would say, "Yes."

And then Uncle Gideon would pop his head in the door and say, "Oh, Derek, there you are! I was wondering where you were. Fliss was too, weren't you, Flissy? We were sure you'd be outside on the beach by now, looking for old bottle caps like you used to do. Remember all those wonderful green ones you found last year?"

After Uncle Gideon had left, I would look over at Derek and whisper, "Uncle Gideon got another letter from my Danny. I know it, but he never lets me see them and he never admits who the letters are from. Do you think that strange? And do you know anything about the piano downstairs with those dreadful nails locking it shut?"

Derek would shake his head against the pillow and say, "I've never seen or heard Gideon play that piano. Flissy, you are stirring up the soup around here."

"Am I?" I said.

I often thought Derek's face looked rather dashing as

he stared at the ceiling. He didn't have to do anything all day. He just lay there listening to music. He told me at least twice that he could never go and ask a girl for a spin on the dance floor. I said it was rubbish. And then he said, "You mean garbage." And I decided all Americans were natural-born teasers and I told Wink so too.

And then one day, another letter arrived from Portugal. I had my hands on it and, as usual, Uncle Gideon grabbed it. And when he went hurrying off into the locked room with it and closed the door behind him, a great idea came into my head.

Danny always said that I was his little bright-idea girl. I'd be sitting on the sofa with him in our lovely flat in London, lying against him, feeling happy and safe with Winnie on the other side of me, embroidering. Danny would pat my head and say, "My little think tank. What are you up to now? What's going on in there?"

And I had to admit that sometimes my ideas could get me into situations. Like the time in London when Winnie and Danny were gone for two days. I wasn't to leave the flat and I wasn't to tell anyone that I was staying there alone. One day, I decided to dry all my blue woolen knickers (underpants) on the railing of the little balcony outside my bedroom. I had them all washed and laid out nicely, when a big wind came up the way it does sometimes in London and it blew all my knickers off the railing and down into the neighbors' walled-in garden next door. And there's no way to get into a walled-in garden like that unless you go down and knock on the neighbor's door, which I did. I said, "Excuse me, my knickers are in your rosebushes. May I go and fetch them?"

★ ☆ ★

My idea involved Derek. And so I went directly to him. I started in by knocking on his door and saying that I had finally finished reading *A Little Princess* by Frances Hodgson Burnett and I wondered if he would like a go at it. He didn't answer and so I opened the door and went into his room and stood there in the dark.

"Derek," I said, speaking right into the shadows. He was lying in bed with his back to me, staring at the wall.

"*Captain* Derek," he said.

"Captain Derek," I said. "Actually, I was rather hoping the captain part was optional."

"Possibly," he said.

"Anyway, another letter has come from Portugal." And now I started whispering. "And Uncle Gideon has got it in that locked room. And oh, Derek, I want so much to see one of the letters. Won't you help me?"

Now Derek was listening. He even rolled over and looked at me. "What do you mean?" he said.

"I need to go in that room," I said. Through the slightly parted curtains, I could see Auntie and The Gram way down the beach, digging for clams. "Now will be a perfect time. I hope you will not think me rude, but I need you to fall out of bed and scream and cry as if you are hurt."

Derek looked pleased. He even sat up.

"And then Uncle Gideon will come rushing in to help you and he'll forget to lock the door."

"Hmmm," Derek said. "You're smart, I see."

"I'm not," I said. "I can't do long division, and Lily Jones says it's ever so simple. Never mind about that. Will you scream and yell? Yes or no."

"Maybe," he said, "but you have to promise to let me see the letters too."

"I won't steal them," I said. "I'll only copy them over. I have a pencil in my pocket and some paper."

"Oh yes, you *are* clever," said Derek, smiling at me. It was the first time that I was to see Derek's smile. And it was a lovely, big, beaming one that went nicely with his grainy, brown-sugar eyes and the sweet music playing in the background. And his smile gave me a British coal fire feeling. I had to close my eyes for a minute because it went through me like British smoke, that delicious smell you breathe in when you are running along the pathways between all the little coal sheds and walled-in gardens behind the row houses in England.

"Thank you ever so much, Derek. Once I see these letters, I promise I won't bother anyone about them again," I said. And I went out into the hall and stood quietly behind a door. I had become quite good at sneaking about this large, dark house full of rifts and lies.

Soon enough, I heard Derek thump out of bed and then begin crying out and calling for help. Just as I hoped, Uncle Gideon came rushing from the locked room, only closing the door behind him, calling out, "Derek, my God, are you all right?"

"Ohhh, I must have broken something," I heard Derek say as I slipped into the unlocked locked room.

British children are not normally nosy or clever or snoopy at all, but I just *had* to know. I had to see those letters.

Once inside, I could see the room was a study, with a globe on a small table and maps on the wall.

Bright, colored thumbtacks on the map of Europe. Books on the desk. Even a copy of *Romeo and Juliet* lying there open.

I quickly searched the drawers and found a small stack of letters, all of them from Portugal and with the blue rectangle in the corner saying BY AIRPLANE. I reached for the first one. The envelope had been carefully slit open. I pulled the letter out and held it up to the light. Then my ears started ringing as if the ocean were roaring inside me. I looked down at the contents. It was all numbers. It read *12-5 21-2-10 64-35 17-7-41-47-110-14. 52-47-46-77-72-16 23-1 80-53-20 70-71-15-5-72-31-53-82* and went on and on. It was quite long and I quickly copied all the numbers over carefully. At the bottom of the page in small letters, it said, *a favorite in Miami.*

My head felt like it was spinning round and round like a boat caught in a whirlpool in the mid Atlantic. I stuffed the paper in my pocket and waited by the door, listening.

I could hear Derek saying, "But I can't move my leg. It really hurts too much."

"Please, Derek," said Gideon, "let's see if I can get you back up in bed and then I will go and call the doctor."

"No, no. No doctor," shouted Derek. But it was too late. Soon I heard Uncle Gideon down on the landing, ringing someone up.

Then I slipped quietly out of the study. I went and stood in a somber way by Derek's bed. He was looking up at me from his pillow. I didn't exactly feel like smiling. I felt confused and shaky. Uncle Gideon was on the phone saying, "Derek, has fallen out of bed. Can you stop over this afternoon?"

"Now you owe me one," said Derek. "I'm going to have to have that doctor poking me again."

"Dreadfully sorry," I said and then I pulled the piece of paper out of my pocket and showed it to Derek.

"Oh, Flissy," he whispered, "oh my goodness. Do you know what this is? The letter is written in code. It's in code!"

★ Sixteen ★

That summer, there were days when the sea was beautiful and calm and green. I could sit on the porch alone in the quiet heat and just stare at the water all afternoon. Oceans can look lovely sometimes, but that loveliness can be deceiving. After all, there were sharks lurking in the water, and German submarines could have easily been prowling about the coast. Why would someone write in code? Why would someone send a letter full of numbers?

That very next evening, I brought up Derek's dinner tray. I opened the door and looked at his bed. It was empty. My eyes rolled round in the dim light. "Derek?" I said. "Have you gone lost on me?"

"No," he said, "not really." There he was, sitting at his desk across the room, no longer wearing pajamas. He was dressed in summer trousers and a striped pullover, looking up the word *code* in his encyclopedia. He was tall and thin and it was nice to be able to see all of him for a change. He kept his one useless arm in his lap.

"People use code when they have a secret. When they don't want anyone to know or see what they have written," he said.

"Because they are hiding something," I said, putting the tray down. "I thought so." My heart sank then like a ship shot full of holes. My Winnie and Danny had lied to me. They were in Portugal, not in London at all. Why did they lie? What were they doing?

"If we want to know what these messages say, we will have to try to figure out how to break the code," Derek said. "And that's going to be very hard because there are as many different codes created as there are birds in the sky or birthdays on the calendar."

We sat there quietly for a long time listening to the wind ruffling and whistling under the shingles on the house, the shutters banging back and forth. We were both thinking about all those strange numbers on that page. If I had been a little starfish caught in a tangle of sea lettuce and kelp, I couldn't have been more discouraged than I felt just now.

Then, to cheer things up and especially because I was rather pleased to see Derek out of bed, I said, "Speaking of birthdays, did you know that the president of the United States, Franklin Roosevelt, has his birthday one day after mine? His birthday is January thirtieth."

"*I* have an assigned birthday," said Derek.

"An assigned birthday?" I said. "And whatever is that?"

"Well," said Derek, "I was assigned a day. It was kind of picked out of a hat for me."

"But doesn't everyone get a birthday naturally when they are born?"

"Yes, but I didn't come with paperwork," he said.

"Well, what day were you assigned, then?" I asked.

"I was assigned January twenty-ninth."

"Oh, but that's *my* birthday," I said. "How very strange. I wonder why. It's not a particularly marvelous sort of day to have for a birthday, is it?"

"Not really," Derek said. "It's just an ordinary day in the middle of winter. Usually very cold outside and sometimes it snows."

"It's not like having a birthday on February twenty-ninth, a leap year," I said. "Then for three years your birthday completely disappears, which could be rather interesting."

"It's because I did not come with paperwork," he said again.

"No paperwork? What do you mean by that?"

"Never mind," said Derek. "I don't like talking about this."

"Oh, nobody likes talking about anything here. I do want to go home," I said. "But I don't know where my passport is or even where my home is because home is where your parents are, and I have misplaced my parents." I had never cried in all my life in front of a handsome, lanky, freckle-faced boy and I wasn't going to start now. So I began trying to count all the bottle caps collected in jars on Derek's desk. I got to 178 and then got all mixed up and was about to start over.

Then Derek said, "Well, look, I'd rather not say this."

"Fine," I said.

"But I'm not actually officially a real Bathburn," he said.

"You're not?" I said, looking up. "You're not Gideon and Miami's little brother?"

"Well, yes I am, and no I'm not. What I mean is, I was adopted and I came with no paperwork. Officially, my real name is Derek Blakely."

"Oh, Derek," I said and I sank to the floor at his feet near the desk, where he was sitting. I felt foggy and glum and sad for him and surprised. I put my hands up to my eyes just in case I might be going to cry this time. "But, Derek, don't you know your *real* mother and your *real* father?"

"No," said Derek, "I don't know anything. I can't remember back that far. I've been here since I was one."

"That's very awful," I said. "I do hope you have lots of friends."

"Well, I do, or I did," he said, "but no one wants anyone coming out to the house now."

"Because you had polio," I said.

"Yes," he said. "But it seems like there are other reasons too. I'm not sure."

Then we sat in the dark room without saying one more word. The house felt suddenly even more somber and gloomy, and my beautiful Winnie and Danny had somehow become lost in the darkness of it.

I had always been good at cheering up quickly. I always was good at thinking of something pleasant or odd, like the way the guards outside of Buckingham Palace never smiled or spoke. They always looked straight ahead as if they were statues, even if you jumped up and down in front of them or touched their hand or asked them where to find the Tower of London.

I squeezed my eyes tight now and hoped something cheeky would come to me in a bright moment. Then I opened them and looked up at Derek. He seemed so tall and clever sitting there with all his code-breaking ideas on paper in front of him.

"Anyway, it doesn't matter about anything. What matters is this," he said and he flung his one useless arm up high. It dropped heavily back to his lap. "I can't help my country and I can't ever ask a girl to dance. And so I'll be staying here in this room. Good-bye." And then he went over to the record player and put on the Bathburns' favorite song again: "I Think of You."

Yes, I am quite good at turning cheerful suddenly, and I can also be rather bold. Winnie said my peculiar boldness always came out of nowhere just when she least expected it. Like one time in London when we were hurrying to the air-raid shelter down in the tube (the subway). We passed a small child on the street all by himself, trudging along slowly. I felt sorry for him, all alone as he was, so I rushed up to him and I grabbed his little hand and pulled him along with us to the shelter.

Now I could feel that strange British boldness coming over me again and there was nothing I could do to stop it. I went over to Derek face-to-face and I said, "You see, you *can* ask a girl for a spin on the dance floor. I'll dance with you. Pick up your left arm and prop it on my shoulder." And I took him by the right hand. He seemed kind of surprised and suddenly we started to do a slow dance, a waltz I think it's called, in the darkened room with "I Think of You" playing.

It felt lovely to dance with Derek. I was thinking, for a boy with no paperwork and an assigned birthday, he was quite nice, really. And then in spite of the letters and the code and the piano and the rift, and even in spite of the war, I rather loved him just then.

★ Seventeen ★

Yes, the ocean in Maine was very loud and the wind was wheezy and wild, but of course, London could be much noisier on the nights when the bombers struck. I would be sleeping in my bed and then we would hear the terrible whine of the air-raid sirens warning us to take cover, to go to the tube for shelter. Sometimes it was too late and we didn't go at all. One night during an air raid, Winnie and Danny and I stood under the staircase in our hall. We were told that the stairwell was the strongest part of the building. Danny was in his slippers. I was barefoot and my feet were cold. So under that stairwell Danny gave me his slippers. I stood there listening to the airplanes droning above us, wearing my Danny's huge, blue, felt slippers. That night, a building down the street was bombed. It was the loudest noise I'd ever heard. We seemed to feel that building collapsing all around us. We smelled dust and smoke. The paintings on the walls in our flat shook and yet, they didn't fall. We lost our electricity for good, but our building was safe.

Later that night when I was in bed again, I heard Winnie and Danny talking. They talked and talked and Winnie cried. When I peeked through my door, I saw my parents sitting together, mostly in the dark except for a small candle flickering on the table. They were talking about something I couldn't understand. It seemed important. Because of that and the bombs, they couldn't keep me in London anymore.

Winnie said, "There's no other choice. We have to take her to your mother's in Maine, darling. You know we must. There's no other alternative."

"I know you're right," said Danny, "but I don't *want* to and I don't know how to approach Gideon after all this time. He's so terribly upset with us. And how would we get there anyway? It's almost impossible to catch a boat to America."

Danny went to the office the next day. It was on Baker Street, the same street where Sherlock Holmes lived in all his books. Winnie seemed very nervous, pacing about while he was gone, embroidering late into the night by candlelight. A few days later, Danny came back from Baker Street looking very sad and cheerful, which was Danny's way, really. He said, "Okay, it's all been figured out. We have a new plan and it's rather extraordinary. A new approach *entirely.*"

And so it was decided. We would be leaving London. I went to Lily Jones's flat to have tea and say good-bye. The whole time I was there, her little brother, Albert, held Wink. He was terribly fond of him and almost cried when I had to take Wink back. Lily Jones put her yellow canary in its pretty cage next to us by the table and for our special good-bye, we ate a whole tin of jam. Then Lily let her canary out of the cage and it was the loveliest thing to see it flying round the room in its brilliant yellow coat, darting this way and that, singing all the while.

The very next day, Winnie and Danny and I took a train. We got the seats with a table in front of us, and Winnie and Danny were drinking ginger beer the whole way. The train was going to Southampton, where the huge boat the HMS *Queen Anne* was leaving the port that night in secret.

★ *Eighteen* ★

A small box arrived at the Bathburn house from overseas in mid-July, and while I didn't actually get to hold it and look at it, I could tell it was from Portugal by the way Uncle Gideon made off with it like a rugby player who finally has his hands on the ball. He tried to make light of it, horsing about in the parlor later, saying he had finally received those shoes he had ordered.

"From Portugal?" I said.

Uncle Gideon winced then and backed up as if a seagull had somehow swooped into the house and had flown too close to his face. Well, that only made me more certain.

I forgot to say that Uncle Gideon was a sixth-grade teacher at the elementary school in town when it wasn't summer, and he was always drinking coffee and shuffling papers, working on his lesson plans. If The Gram asked him to tidy up the kitchen after tea, he always said, "Sorry, old thing, school's starting soon and I've got work here," and then he'd wave his papers about. (As soon as I got to Bottlebay, he started calling *everybody* "old thing.")

"Shall we eat on the porch, old thing?" I heard him say to The Gram a little later. We were going to be having Grammy's Clammy Stew for dinner. It was a great Bathburn favorite. For me, I couldn't believe how much food was in Bottlebay, Maine. In London, we'd had very little to eat. And I was wondering all the while in a wistful sort of way *what* my parents would have sent to Uncle Gideon. And why was there nothing for me?

I was sitting upstairs with Derek in the dark bedroom. He had a pencil behind his ear and a pad of paper on his desk. He was looking at me and thinking out loud. "The first thing we have to do before we figure out the code is figure out what 'a favorite in Miami' is," he said. "Hmmmm, do you think they mean Miami, Florida? And what sort of things are favorites in Florida... seashells? Pink flamingoes?"

"Derek," I said, looking over to see if he was willing for me to drop the Captain part. "Derek," I went on. "I have been thinking and thinking. It can't be Miami, Florida. It has to be Miami Bathburn. Aunt Miami."

"Oh, of course. Of course," said Derek. "Flissy, you are showing brilliance."

"Don't forget the long division," I said.

"Oh, right," he said. I got another Derek-coal-fire smile then, the kind that tingled all through me and went straight to my toes and then came swimming back round to the top of my head.

"What would be a favorite with Miami?" said Derek. He was whispering now, which was a good thing because suddenly Uncle Gideon was casting a heavyhearted shadow out in the hall. It was a large shadow and fell across the floorboards and stopped just at Derek's doorway. Uncle Gideon paused, then took a few steps backwards. He seemed to be listening and watching all the time and then looking at me as if I'd just jumped out from behind a door and surprised him. He never seemed to get used to my face.

"Hello, Fliss, how are you? Okay? It's time to eat. It's a great summer evening. You'll like this stew, I think, I hope. We haven't had a dinner on the porch in ages. What do you say, Derek? Do you think we can drag him out of there, Fliss, you and I, as a team? You pull on one leg and I'll pull on the other? What do you say? We've never done anything together. We might be unstoppable, you know."

I folded my arms in front of me. Some of Uncle Gideon's jokes were very flat and childish, I thought. "I daresay Derek won't want to come out at all," I said.

"What, Flissy? Don't be silly," said Derek. He had hidden the paper with the numbers on it when he heard Uncle Gideon's voice in the hallway, and now he put several books on top of the paper and looked over at me. Then he stood up and walked across his room as if nothing had been wrong in the first place.

Derek paused at the threshold of his door. I waited. Uncle Gideon waited. Down below, The Gram and Miami waited. Derek looked over at me and I looked back at him. There was a split second when the whole house seemed to stop; even the wind was quiet for a moment. And then after weeks and weeks of being in his room, Derek set out towards the landing.

When he got to the top of the stairs, there was a rousing cheer from Auntie, Uncle Gideon, and The Gram. And I joined in, of course. We all clapped and called and cheered with every step Derek took towards the porch.

Downstairs, Uncle Gideon patted Derek on the back. I thought perhaps Uncle Gideon had a cold, because his eyes were all wet and he got out his handkerchief.

We sat on the porch at a table, looking at the sea. This evening it was rolling in and out in a calm, quiet way, reminding me of a lion that was taking a nap for a moment. There was a beautiful pink sunset wrapped round the sky.

Auntie Miami stood up before we ate and said she wanted to do her favorite Juliet lines just one more time. "I know. I know. You've all heard it before. Perhaps I *am* a bit of a dreamer, but *he's* much worse than I am." She pointed to Uncle Gideon, who closed his eyes and took the punch without retaliating. "But it *is* a lovely part and I did so want to play that role," she said. "Do you really think I would make a good Juliet?"

"You have great stage presence," said Uncle Gideon. "You really do. When you are in a room, *no one* sees anyone but you. Isn't that so, Derek?"

Aunt Miami smiled softly.

So with the sky darkening and churning like a stew being stirred, and the smell of salt and clam chowder in the air, she began, *"O Romeo, Romeo, wherefore art thou Romeo?"*

And suddenly, Derek and I both perked up at the same moment, I looking once again into his brown, winsome eyes. Suddenly, we both knew what "a favorite in Miami" was. We both wanted to jump up and shout, "That's it! That's it. We've got it!!!"

Nineteen

Well, we hadn't exactly cracked the code, but we knew now that Auntie's favorite lines would help. So when Auntie and Uncle Gideon were doing the dishes later, singing together at the top of their lungs in the kitchen, Derek went into the library quietly and snatched Auntie's copy of *Romeo and Juliet*. Just as he was leaving the library, The Gram caught him up and gave him a hug and said, "So glad you decided to join the land of the living, dear."

Soon enough, Derek slipped upstairs and copied over those lines, Auntie's favorites.

O Romeo, Romeo, wherefore art thou Romeo?
Deny thy father and refuse thy name,
Or, if thou wilt not, be but sworn my love,
And I'll no longer be a Capulet.

I hung over him as he worked, thinking how smart he was and how glad I was that we had the same birthday. I was thinking perhaps we could have a joint birthday party on the day before President Roosevelt had his celebration. We'd have to have two birthday cakes, I thought, because Derek liked chocolate and I didn't. Well, I wouldn't mind a chocolate birthday cake with vanilla icing, if that's what Derek wanted. I could eat just the icing. I'd have done anything for Derek, really. Of course, I didn't want him to know that, because he might then have sent me on all sorts of dreadful errands.

Just now, Derek was saying, "You know, Danny and Gideon used to write notes to each other in code when they were boys. I mean years and years before I was here."

"They did?" I said.

"Yes, they did," said Derek.

"Well, then," I said, "that makes sense, doesn't it."

I was thinking how super Derek was to be helping me with the code. He had even taken a flashlight with him to bed to study the numbers in the letter. He was also reading *King Arthur and the Knights of the Round Table* late at night with that flashlight. And he had made a rather big drawing of Sir Gawain. He said he wanted to be like him when he grew up, except Sir Gawain would not have had a paralyzed arm.

"Now that I have the lines written out, we'll be able to hold the numbers up and see if anything comes to us," said Derek. "Keep thinking about these lines, Flissy, even when you're sleeping. Sometimes you can figure out things in dreams."

I looked at him when he was turned away and couldn't see me. I was wondering what his dreams were like at night. I wanted to float above him then and scatter sweet dreams on his pillow as he slept.

★ ☆ ★

For that whole morning, Auntie's favorite lines seemed to repeat inside my head. And later, when The Gram and I were doing our cleaning rounds, those lines seemed to follow me about. We started with Aunt Miami's room. My job was to pull off all the pillowcases and stuff the fat pillows into clean, fresh ones. I opened the windows and drew back the curtains.

Winnie and Danny had been too busy to do any cleaning in London. We had a housekeeper who took care of everything in our flat. I wasn't at all used to this sort of thing. I was feeling very much like the Little Princess just now, the way she had to work all the time carrying coal about in buckets in the snow. I wasn't working *terribly* hard, actually. In fact, I was up on the mattress lying flat on my back, enjoying the cool, clean, new cotton sheet. Then I started trying to stand on my head, but I kept falling over.

The Gram said, "Flissy dear, I can't put on the top sheet unless you move. Practice that on the floor for a moment, will you?" So I jumped off the bed, trying to land on the hooked rug The Gram had made and I did. I jumped smack onto the center of a woolen hand-hooked rose. I was thinking about those Juliet lines, but not wanting The Gram to know, I started whistling, which I'm not very good at.

As I was whistling, I looked about on Auntie's dressing table at some of her photographs and pressed flowers and things like that. There, lying next to a lilac-colored jewelry box, was a journal. The Gram was shaking out a new clean top sheet for Miami's bed. It lifted and billowed up above her like a great white parachute and then, as it floated down towards the bed, for just one moment, I opened Auntie's journal.

It read, "*Oh, will I ever meet anyone in this wretched lonely place?*" Then the sheet was down and The Gram was tucking it in and I closed the journal.

"Busy, busy, busy," said The Gram just then as she

spread the sheet tightly round the mattress. "Too busy to take a side and tuck?"

I went over to help her. But the whole time after that, I was feeling sad for Auntie because she was lonely and wanted to have a husband and be married. So I said to The Gram, "Does Auntie ever go on dates to the movies and all that?"

"Flissy, you are full of bright ideas," said The Gram. "Are you ready to move on to Derek's room? Will you carry the laundry basket? And if you happen to meet up with an eligible bachelor, send him along our way, will you?"

I was going to ask her what she meant exactly by "an eligible bachelor" but she'd already moved on, leaving me to drag the big, heavy laundry basket across the hall. I was huffing and puffing and thinking again of the Little Princess and feeling just like her, so *terribly* over-worked, except that I wasn't covered in coal, and my clothes weren't all raggedy and torn. But I had the same miserable sad look on my face. I stopped and looked in the mirror outside of Derek's room. I tilted my head so that I looked even more sorry and tired.

Derek was on the floor, cutting out a shield for Sir Gawain with his one good hand. Luckily, it was his left that got all paralyzed. Still, it's very hard to do all sorts of things with only one hand. For instance, how do you put tooth powder on a toothbrush with only one hand? How do you put on a glove? How do you open a bottle of root beer?

The Gram and I took his sheets off his bed. Then I went over to the windows and pulled the cords, and the curtains slipped away and all kinds of bright summer light filled Derek's room. I looked over at Derek. He just went on cutting out Sir Gawain's shield. Then he held up Sir Gawain's sword that he had made out of shirt card- board and glued-on glitter. He pointed it towards the ceiling, and the sun came through the fluttering leaves outside and shone on Derek's sparkling sword. Then I thought he looked so handsome, so ferocious, so daring, and so sweet that I felt rather giddy, or dizzy, as they say here in America.

The Gram went trotting off to hang laundry outside with Miami, and I was left to bring down the basket of sheets. When I got downstairs, I noticed there was some- one at the front door. Through the curtains, I could see quite clearly it was a policeman. In England we call them bobbies and they carry wooden clubs on their belts. The American policeman was wearing a gun and holster, reminding me of the cowboys I had expected to find when I got to America.

The policeman was knocking loudly, and suddenly I appeared to be all alone downstairs.

"Aunt Miami," I called out in the hallway. No one answered. No one was in the kitchen either, and Uncle Gideon wasn't in the library. I knew Derek was upstairs in his room, but I also knew he wasn't always keen on leaving it, so I went myself to the door.

"Hello," I said, peering out at the policeman.

"Is Mr. Bathburn here?" said the policeman.

"No, I don't believe he is at the moment," I said. "Is everything all right?"

"Perhaps," he said. "I'm just coming down from the White Whale Inn. Just checking around about something."

"Oh," I said. I looked out the side window, and I could now see The Gram and Aunt Miami in the garden, hanging laundry. Miami's cotton dresses danced this way and that on the clothesline. "My grandmother is out there," I said, looking towards the garden, which the Bathburns called the yard.

"Okay, thanks," he said, walking off the porch and going round to the north side of the house. Through the lace at the window on the side, I could see The Gram's face full of darkness, even in the sunlight. And Auntie too was looking down. I watched the policeman talking with them, gesturing and pointing among all those dresses and shirts and towels and white sheets that were flapping and flying in the wind.

★ Twenty ★

Sometimes ideas can come out of nowhere, as if they simply drop from the sky. Like last week, when a skinny loaf of bread fell from the clouds and landed on the sand in front of Aunt Miami and me as if by magic. We couldn't imagine where that loaf had come from. Finally, we looked up and saw a seagull circling above us, waiting to pick up the loaf of bread he had just dropped.

In that very way, an idea came to me out of the blue the next afternoon. I was thinking about Winnie and Danny and the day they brought me to Bottlebay, Maine. After turning away and refusing to speak to Danny for a while, Uncle Gideon had finally gone off for a walk down the beach with him. They took something in a large box with them. The Gram had never asked Winnie into the house that day, so Winnie had sat with me on the porch with her arm round me. She was crying and hugging me. I just lay against her shoulder being very quiet. It's always that way when someone cries about you. You just sort of wait till its over, not really knowing what to do. I sat there feeling terribly important and terribly sad all at the same time. Then Winnie clicked open her purse. She had a pair of white gloves in there, and her purse smelled of face powder and lipstick. She pulled out a plain sealed envelope. She didn't say anything about it. She just hugged me and we let the swing rock gently like a cradle.

Then Danny and Uncle Gideon were coming back. Winnie had said to me, "It's a good thing they're patching things up. When you see a real war, suddenly you want to stop with your own petty battles, don't you? And Danny has missed everyone so terribly."

Just now I was remembering seeing Danny and Uncle Gideon going off together down the beach. It was a blurry memory and only now when I thought of it, I seemed to recall that when they came back that afternoon, they didn't have the box with them.

Then I remembered how Winnie had quietly handed me the envelope. "Can you do something very grown up for me?" she had said. "Can I trust you not to open this? Will you give it to Uncle Gideon a week before Christmas? Promise?"

I had taken the sealed envelope and stuffed it under my suitcase in the closet so I wouldn't be tempted to peek, because British children are very trustworthy. I only looked at the outside of the envelope now and again and quickly stuffed it away.

I was remembering it all clearly now as I sat in the window seat in the hallway upstairs at the front of the house. The sunlight was dropping across my lap, and I was lining up a row of English pennies and ha'pennies that I brought from England, making a lovely design with them amongst the velvet-covered buttons on the window seat cushion. Then I looked out the window. Uncle Gideon was taking his long walk down the beach alone. I studied his back as he moved along, leaving footprints in the sand behind him. They made a zigzag pattern, and I noticed he was carrying a folder under his arm.

I decided to go outside. There was a hot summer wind blowing across the water, and I walked up into the sandy grass next to the house on the ridge, thinking about that folder. I picked some stray wildflowers that were growing in a protected area near the road. All the while, the clouds above piled up in great white mountains against the blue sky and then were knocked down and spread out by the wind.

I brought the wildflower bouquet back into the house and found a jar in the kitchen and filled it with water.

"Busy. Busy. Busy, as usual, Flissy," said The Gram as I passed the pantry.

I took the bouquet up to Derek's room. He was at his desk. I set the bouquet on a little table.

"What have you got, Flissy?" he said, looking out from behind the cover of his book, which showed a knight rushing forward with a sword.

"Oh, just something for you that I picked," I said, turning in a circle. He lowered his book a little more. He sat up very tall. His cheeks went ever so slightly pink. He cleared his throat and then he looked round at *everything* in the room, except the bouquet.

I skipped quickly out into the hall. I skipped up and down along the banister and then I ended up sitting in the window seat again.

The sun had changed positions now and was lying on the floor, making a bright yellow square at my feet. I looked out the window and saw Uncle Gideon on the beach, coming back now towards the house. I noticed with a jolt that he was no longer carrying the folder and *that* was when another great idea came into my head.

Twenty-One

A great idea should always be left to steep like loose tea leaves in a teapot for a while, to make sure that the tea will be strong enough and that the idea truly is a great one. And so I let my idea rest for a day or two before telling Derek anything.

The next day, I was sitting on the sofa with Auntie Miami. I was watching her stitches as she hemmed a skirt. I had to look very closely so I could see how long each stitch was.

Finally, Aunt Miami said, "Whatever are you looking at?"

"I'm studying your stitches and I am trying to measure how long they are," I said. "Because in England, we have to sew in school, and the smaller the stitches, the higher the points you get. I'm looking to see if you should get a star."

"Oh, Flissy, you are a funny duck," said Auntie Miami.

"And I'm not a duck. I don't have a bill and I don't

go around quacking." I leaned my head on her shoulder and looked at her stitches even more carefully. And then I said, "Auntie, what is it that Uncle Gideon and my Danny fought over? It must have been a terrible fight for Danny to stay away twelve long years. And to cause such a *rift*."

"Yes, it was," said Auntie Miami. "It was a terrible fight."

"And what did they fight about?" I said.

"Oh, Flissy, why aren't you off playing with dolls like other girls at your age?"

"Well, I had a few dolls in England, but I never really fancied them. I chose Wink when I packed my suitcases before we left. Of course I would always be faithful to Wink. I'd have stayed in London and let bombs fall on my head if Wink had to be left behind, even if I am too old now for a bear."

"Flissy, you are a card. Did you know that?"

"What did they fight about?" I said again.

"I should not tell you any of this, but it was about love, of course," Auntie Miami whispered. "It's always about love."

"Is it?" I said.

"Yes, Gideon and Danny were in college in England, at Oxford, and they both loved the same girl."

"Oh," I said, "how sad."

"In fact, Gideon knew her first and she was his girl-friend. Then Danny met her and fell deeply in love with her, and she with him."

"Oh, how terrible," I said. "Poor Uncle Gideon."

"Yes, it was very sad. He took it very hard. He left school, came back to America, wouldn't come out of his room for almost a month."

"Poor Uncle Gideon," I said again. "And who was the girl they both loved?"

Auntie Miami put down her sewing. She looked at me for a long time. She seemed to have an answer all over her face, but it was an answer without words. Finally, she said, "Don't you know who it was?"

And I said, "No."

And then she looked at me very hard again and waited.

"Oh," I said, "was it my mum, Winnie?"

"Yes," said Auntie, "yes, it was."

I looked up at the ceiling then, following the cracks to see if they made any pictures. I could almost see a big, lopsided, sorrowful heart up there, or else it was a dog's head without ears. I wondered what kind of dog wouldn't have ears. And then I said, "Uncle Gideon hasn't married anyone yet?"

And Auntie Miami said, "No, he hasn't even gone on a date since then. He still keeps her in his heart. He still loves her."

"Very much?" I said.

"Very, very much," she said.

"And you said in your diary, 'Oh, will I ever meet anyone in this wretched lonely place?' " I said.

"Felicity Budwig Bathburn. How did you read that?"

"I didn't mean to, honestly," I said. "I didn't want to. It just fell open when I was helping The Gram clean your room."

"Flissy B. Bathburn, why aren't you off playing with dolls?" she said again.

"I told you, I don't have any and besides I'm faithful to Wink. I'm steadfast and true to Wink forever."

And then I started thinking about Uncle Gideon and my mum, Winnie, and my dad, Danny, and I listened to the ocean crashing against the rocks and the wind pushing sand through the cracks in the windows, and from upstairs in Derek's room, I could hear a record playing. It was one of those sad little jazzy songs.

★ Twenty-Two ★

I always tried to avoid *Life* magazine when it came in on
Wednesdays. The photographs always bothered me.
Today, there were pictures on the cover of Nazi airplanes
barreling across the sky in Europe and formations below
of soldiers marching with those terrible red and black
swastikas on their armbands. I looked away. I was thinking about what Aunt Miami had told me about the fight
between the Bathburn brothers. I understood now why
Uncle Gideon had pushed Danny away when we first got
here and why he wouldn't speak to Winnie. And *in that
way* I did feel bad for Uncle Gideon. In that way. Still,
because of the letters and that package, all these foggy
images were swimming past me now like silent U-boats.
Life magazine said that groups of Nazi submarines trav-
eled in what they called Wolf Packs. The very name
made me shiver.

All day after talking with Aunt Miami, I tried,
really and truly tried, *not* to think about that fight.
But now that I knew more, the envelope Winnie had
given me in great trust that day on the porch seemed

to float before my eyes. Every time I turned round, it felt like the envelope was almost hovering over my head. I looked in the hall mirror to see if it was really there. But it wasn't. Then I ended up making faces at myself in the mirror just for fun.

Uncle Gideon walked by and said, "What ho, Fliss!" He put two rabbit ears behind my head with his two fingers and then he said, "Still British, are you? Haven't lost the accent, have you?" I tried to smile at him. Honestly I did.

I went out on the porch to fetch Wink, who was lying on the floor in the sunlight. Uncle Gideon followed me out there and leaned down and put his sunglasses on Wink and then he went to get a towel and set him on it. "Look, Flissy, he's sunbathing!" he said. "What do you think? Miami, come out and see what has become of Wink. He's a movie star now!" Then Uncle Gideon got out his Brownie box camera and took pictures of Wink. He thought it was the funniest thing in the world, Wink in sunglasses, sunbathing.

I just didn't know what to think about anything. I leaned against the porch railing, waiting until he was finished. I kept thinking as I watched him that he loved my Winnie. He still loved her very much.

Derek was nearby on the porch swing, reading again.

I too had a book under my arm, *The Secret Garden* by Frances Hodgson Burnett, and I was planning to become an authority on her. Finally, when Uncle Gideon went into the house and started chasing Miami about with his camera, I sat down with my book on the floor near Wink. I was singing "Once in Royal David's City" to myself.

"A Christmas song on a beautiful summer day, Flissy?" Derek said, looking right at me. "You've got a good voice, though."

"Did you hate the bouquet I brought you? Awfully, terribly, horribly?" I said, trying to count Derek's freckles on the bridge of his nose as I talked. When I got to eight, I decided, with freckles, it was better to just guess.

"Flissy," he said, smiling, "while you've been singing, have you thought up any new ways to crack a code?"

"Hmm," I said, "perhaps. Maybe." I had been waiting to tell him my great idea. I had been hoping Winnie would ring me up and explain, so we wouldn't have to continue guessing. It would often be like that in London. Danny and Winnie would be gone when I came home from school. They'd be gone hours into the night, and I would sit at the window without moving at all, waiting in the darkness, worrying and wondering.

Then the telephone would ring and it would be Winnie.

"All I can think of," said Derek, "is if Gideon is getting these letters and they are addressed to him, he must understand the code. So the way to crack the code is through him."

"Yes, Derek," I said spinning round and round until everything seemed upside down and all mixed up. "And I've been wanting to say that I *do* have an idea."

I went over to Derek. He was leaning his head back on the porch swing, thinking. I went up close and whispered to him, "Uncle Gideon often goes on a long walk and he carries a folder with him. Sometimes he doesn't bring the folder back. I honestly think we ought to *follow* him."

The sun seemed to drop just a tiny bit lower on the horizon so that a shaft of light now fell directly across Derek's face. Or perhaps I was wrong; perhaps his face just lit up because he was very pleased with my idea.

★ Twenty-Three ★

I didn't imagine that I could get Derek to leave the house actually. I mean he was on the porch swing all the time, but so far he hadn't even been down the long steps to stick his toes in the ocean. He was awfully self-conscious about his arm. Even though recently, Auntie Miami had made him a sling to cover it up. And Derek didn't want to go back to school. I heard him having a row with The Gram the night before. He was saying he was not going back, no matter what, and The Gram was saying he had to.

And I was going to have to go to school as well. The strangest part of all was that I was going to have Uncle Gideon as my sixth-grade teacher. Which made me ever so nervous because I didn't want anyone at school to know about Wink. I wasn't at all sure that Uncle Gideon wouldn't tease me about him. All the girls might be talking about nail varnish and new hairdos and Uncle Gideon might mention Wink and then I would have to be transferred to another school in another country altogether, like Portugal perhaps. And immediately.

I got out some paper to write again to Winnie. I was feeling almost like shouting out extremely loudly, "Why is there no proper mailing address for you, Winnie?" I'm sorry to say that I hit my pillow. Then I threw the pillow across the room.

Dear Winnie,

I am not at all angry at you for leaving me here and not explaining what you are doing. Honestly. I don't mind feeling terribly lost and alone and worried. Truly. And I do like writing letters and not mailing them. Honestly.

Love, love, love,

Your Felicity

I went across my little tower room to pick up the pillow. I punched it and threw it again. Then I took a couple of books and stomped on their spines, ripping the pages. Wink sat there staring at me. "Oh, Wink I *am* sorry," I said. "I shouldn't have done that."

Then I looked out my window and saw Mr. Henley coming down the hill with his big fat mail pouch. I looked at his hopeful face, and most of my anger just sort of cracked apart like waves when they hit the rocky shore. Each piece of jagged anger sank away into nothingness.

The mail pouch looked fatter than usual and the postman was smiling and I could just tell he had a real letter for us again. So I opened my window and shouted, "Hello, Mr. Henley. Are you pleased about something?"

He smiled and waved and I shot down the stairs like Derek's toy cannon. I think I broke a world record getting down the stairs, trying to beat Uncle Gideon. But Gideon wasn't even nearby and neither was The Gram. Perhaps they had gone off in the Packard for supplies in town.

I got down on the beach and just about threw myself in front of Mr. Henley. He really looked very topping and he had a letter for us and it was one of the ones in code. I could tell. The envelope was ever so light and delicate with a red-and-blue airmail design round the border. I took the letter in my hand like it was spun sugar, like one of Winnie's elaborate cake decorations that she used to make sometimes on her days off before the war. I tried somehow to hold the letter without touching it, if that was possible.

Suddenly, my pillow-punching mood disappeared entirely and I looked at Mr. Henley and I said, "Have you been married very long, Mr. Henley?"

"I'm not married at all," he said, and he slapped the side of his mail pouch. "Too busy, I suppose."

"What a pity," I said and I tried to look very sorrowful. "Well, thank you ever so much for the letter."

I tore back up the steps as if I were a cannonball being propelled by a rubber band in one of Derek's battles, which made me think of one of Derek's soldiers, the broken one that reminded me of the sad little tin soldier in the Grimm fairy tale.

When I got back up the long stairs, I went into the dining room, where Derek was sitting with a deck of cards. He loved to play hearts. All the Bathburns did. I slipped the thin letter up my sleeve and I sat at the other side of the table and looked at Derek. I tried to be very ho-hum and not act excited at all about the letter. I put my elbows on the table and leaned my chin in my hands and I just sat there watching Derek. He had such lovely posture. He would have made a tremendous knight, I thought just then, if he had lived long ago in England near, say, Goodrich Castle in Herefordshire.

Derek and I played a round of hearts. You can play with two people, but you have to make a dummy hand. And the whole time we played, I had the letter inside my sleeve. It felt very itchy and I was sure that's why I lost the game. The day before, I lost because there was a fly buzzing round my head and I couldn't think properly, and the day before that, I lost because I was hungry. In fact, I'd never won at hearts since I'd been in Bottlebay, Maine. I almost beat The Gram on Saturday. She appeared to be losing, but then at the very last, she had all the best cards. That's when I had decided to lie down on the floor and pretend I was floating in the ocean. The Gram had said, "Oh, Flissy, don't pout. You'll get the hang of it. The Bathburns always win at hearts. The card game, that is."

Derek was trying to prop several cards in his one miserable paralyzed hand now, but the cards just fell from his fingers and scattered about. Then Derek dropped his head and shoulders down so that his cheek was lying now on the tabletop. "It's not fair," he said. "How am I supposed to discard and draw when I am already holding a handful of cards? And I'm not going to go back to school either."

"I should think you'd be feeling rather smug right now, having just won at hearts again," I said. And while Derek was moaning and groaning, I pulled the letter slowly out of my sleeve and I set it on the table right near Derek's nose.

Derek sat up. "Where did you get this, Flissy?" he asked.

"It came today in the mail," I said. "Uncle Gideon must have gone to town with The Gram for groceries and missed it."

"We'd better not open it," said Derek, "but there's no harm in holding it up to the light." With his good arm, Derek held the envelope up to the window. But we couldn't see through it. It seemed to stare back at us in silence. I traced my fingers over the address and Danny's handwriting. It felt quite nice, really, to be so close to something Danny had written not long before. And then my heart got heavy again because he hadn't written to me. It sank just as if it weighed six stones five, the very weight of Jillian Osgood before she even entered the fifth form.

"Let's try leaving the letter here on the table and see what Uncle Gideon does about it. See if he goes anywhere, so we can follow him," I said and I put my hands on my hips and I scrunched up my nose to show that I was quite serious.

And Derek said, "Flissy, if they had horses and cattle and cowboy boots and lassos and campfires and Wyoming in England, you'd be a true British cowgirl."

Twenty-Four

We went into the hall and got into the closet to hide. I had said, "Shall we get in the cupboard?"

And Derek had said, "That's not a cupboard, it's a closet, and yes, let's." Quite cleverly, we left the door open just a crack. Through that crack we could see the dining room table and the letter lying there. Derek said, "At school, Roland Rupert shut himself in his locker once because he didn't want to take a math test. Those lockers lock by themselves when you shut the door, you know. And Roland was in there all afternoon."

"But how did he ever get out?" I asked.

"When he didn't come home at two thirty, his mother had them search the school, and when they opened his locker, Roland Rupert rolled out. That's what I'll do if they make me go back to school," said Derek.

"I wonder if there's room for two in your American lockers," I said.

We were all stuffed under a row of wool coats and I was sitting on some old rubber boots, with a fuzzy cape draped over my shoulders. Derek put on a big wool hat with fur-lined earflaps, the one he said Uncle Gideon always wore in the winter when he went to the Shriners Club. Then Derek buckled his feet into some enormous snowshoes, which caused me to get a bit of a laughing attack, which then caused us both to fall into the back of the closet. When we got straightened out, I ended up quite close to Derek, looking at his nice, soft, land-of-counterpane eyes, and even in the semidarkness, it felt as if I were in a little airplane hovering over the surface of Derek's face, roaming over his brown eyelashes, skimming lightly across his handsome forehead.

Just then, we heard voices on the steps outside, and Derek tried to get up, but he kept falling back into the depths of the stuffed closet, laughing. Finally, it was me who got to my feet and watched The Gram and Uncle Gideon carry bags into the kitchen. It was me who saw Uncle Gideon notice the envelope on the table in the dining room. It was me who heard Uncle Gideon call out, "What did you say, Mother? You unpack the canned goods. I think I'll go up to my room and then I'll take a walk while the sun's high." He picked up the letter, went upstairs, unlocked the study, and went in, clicking the door shut behind him.

Twenty-Five

Uncle Gideon seemed to be taking his time in the study. Looking out through the crack and waiting for him to come back, I felt a bit like a jar full of crickets. My hands were jumping about on their own. I tried to glare at them in a fierce sort of way to get them to stop, but they kept on going. Derek was lying on a pile of sweaters, snoring. He was faking, of course. As he lay there, I thought he looked so much like that little tin soldier with the missing arm and the sad smile, the one who wanted to be just like the others and tried so hard and had such a lovely heart.

What was Uncle Gideon going to do with this new letter and how long would he be? What would we do or say if by chance he should stop by the closet for a hat? In the kitchen, The Gram and Auntie Miami were unpacking groceries from bags. I could hear cans being stacked and the icebox door being opened. The Gram was saying, "Well, if Flissy is a little immature for her age, I wouldn't blame her. I would be too, given her unstable situation. Under these circumstances, Winifred had no business having a child in the first place. And then to be so neglectful and selfish."

I was hoping I had been mixed up and heard that all wrong. Perhaps they were talking about someone else named Winifred and not my lovely Winnie. I wanted to shout out loudly again, "No, that's not so. The Gram is wrong. I *know* she's wrong. You're wrong." I closed my eyes and I pinched my lips shut with my fingers so I couldn't say a word.

"Fliss," said Derek. He tilted his head and looked at me up close. "Are you upset? Come on," he said, putting on a partly smashed black bowler hat, the kind all the businessmen in London wear, minus the smash. "Don't be sad."

Just then, we heard Uncle Gideon coming down the stairs. Derek and I waited silently, watching through the crack as Uncle Gideon passed quickly by, holding in his arms a plain brown folder.

Twenty-Six

Uncle Gideon already had a good start on us because it took a few minutes getting out of the hats and capes and snowshoes. As we were creeping out of the closet, The Gram was still talking with Auntie. She was saying something like "Well, they were only married three months and then it was over, from Winifred's perspective. I can't understand how one woman could wreak such havoc with my sons. Did you put the mayonnaise away, dear?"

I wasn't sure what "wreaking havoc" meant, but I wanted to go into the kitchen right then and shout out, "I awfully, terribly, dreadfully hate hearing you say any bad things about my Winnie!"

I was about to leap towards the kitchen when Derek gently pulled on my arm. "Fliss," he said, "now's our chance. Come on." He motioned to me to be quiet and to follow him, which I did. All the while, The Gram's words were tumbling about in my head.

We slipped out on the porch and looked off towards

the beach below. There was Gideon scooting along. We hurried down the steps, doing two at a time.

When we got to the beach, the sand was clean and wet and firm, once again the best conditions for making very nice footprints, and Uncle Gideon was leaving perfect ones behind him as he walked.

We decided to step only in Uncle Gideon's footprints so that no one would ever know that we had been following him. His footprints were big (my print took up less than one half of his), and they were far apart so that I had to leap sometimes to make it to the next print. Derek did it too, and one time he tripped over me and we both fell onto the sand, having another laughing fit. It was nice to see Derek outside lying on his back, looking up at the clouds, laughing. It seemed as if he had forgotten all about his paralyzed arm for a moment. I was laughing too, as if The Gram hadn't just said all those terrible things about my Winnie, which was good because when you can't do anything about something, it is better to try to forget all about it.

We had lost Gideon completely by now. He had gone quite far down the beach, moving at a fast pace, and had taken a turn away from the water towards land. We were able to follow his footprints right to a forest path, which cut across the point. There in the brush we lost the footprints, but we followed the path anyway, all the way to the other side of the woods.

Derek was looking rather pleased and energetic, like a hunting dog happy to be out running, one of those lovely brown and white springer spaniels with long legs, the kind Winnie grew up with in Devonshire. He looked so interested that I took the opportunity to say, "Derek, do you think I could have the little tin soldier with the missing arm, the one who's got chipped paint on part of his uniform? He's so much sweeter than the others."

"Well, he's my mapmaker," said Derek. "I kind of need him. Look where we are now. Look up, Flissy."

And I did look up and we had reached the edge of the woods and we were on a bluff covered in wild yellow flowers. The sky was a pure, drop-away, British blue, the same blue on the British flag, the same blue in one of Winnie's summer dresses, the same blue as the sky above the Long Man of Wilmington in East Sussex County, England. There was one big, fat, white cloud puffing along that looked a bit like Wink floating across the sky, wondering why he was always left behind these days.

I could hear the ocean, which *was* rougher on this side, but until we got to the top of the bluff, I couldn't see it, and then we went over a rise amidst hundreds of windy yellow flowers and there it was, way down below at the bottom of the cliff, the true blue, forceful, crashing ocean that makes all creatures in every corner of the world feel small and shivery and lonely in a terrible, lovely sort of way.

The drop-off made me take a deep breath. My feet felt light, like they might lift up and away into the air, and I tried to push down on them so that they would stay put. There was a steep path that wound down the bluff and I could see, far below, a short wooden dock and a small open boat, and Uncle Gideon was in that boat, starting the motor.

"I guess he's going to Peace Island," said Derek. "It's over there. It's like a bird sanctuary, covered in cliffs of nesting plovers, sandpipers, puffins, seagulls, and blue herons." Derek looked all shadowy for a moment, as if the sun suddenly had gone behind a cloud, taking the color out of everything. "There's nothing over there," he said. "Nothing except birds and fields of long grass and rocky cliffs. Because of those jagged bluffs and the heavy wind over there, it's considered dangerous. As far as I know, nobody ever goes to Peace Island."

Twenty-Seven

From where we were, we could watch Uncle Gideon as his boat moved towards the island. We saw him dock the boat and climb the path up the cliff. We sat crouched there in the scratchy yellow flowers for ever so long. "If we only had a boat," I said.

"The mailman has one," said Derek. "He talks about it all the time. He was painting it last summer and apologized about a big blue thumbprint on the newspaper he handed me."

"I see," I said, "but if you mean Mr. Henley, he's off delivering mail right now, isn't he." I rolled over onto my back among the leaves, trying to stay out of the sun. I wanted to lie there in the flowers forever. I didn't want to go back to that big house full of whispering. I wanted to *know* what was going on. Did Winnie and Danny need some kind of help? Were they in danger? My face was beginning to feel sunburned, and my arms were turning pink. My head felt cloudy and light.

"Did you hate my bouquet really and truly?" I said again to Derek, picking one of the yellow flowers near me. "And by the way, Derek, do you say bucks or dollars?"

Derek looked a bit confused for a moment and then his face cleared and he smiled. "Oh, I say bucks. Can you loan me five bucks?"

"I thought so," I said.

"We need to get you out of the sun, Flissy," Derek said, "unless you want to turn into a cooked lobster."

"I am starving," I said.

"Me too," he said.

"I could eat a horse. Could you? Could you easily eat something that enormous right now, even with those great big hooves?"

"Yup," said Derek. "I could. Easily."

"Me too," I said. Then I closed my eyes and tried to look terribly hungry and sad.

"Fliss, don't die on me. Are you okay? Wake up," said Derek.

I opened one eye and looked at Derek. I kept the other eye closed and gloomy because I liked it when Derek tried to cheer me up. In fact, I liked everything about Derek. The problem was, I was beginning to worry that he didn't *like* me back.

★ ☆ ★

As we were walking along later, I was wondering to myself again why Winnie and Danny would send a letter all full of numbers and why Uncle Gideon would take that letter in a folder to a wild island full of birds. If only there had been a note on the outside of the envelope for me, saying something like "I love you, little think tank."

I decided I had more nicknames than any girl in the USA and I had the longest name in the world too. Felicity Bathburn Budwig took three full seconds to say, which was much longer than most children's names. Lily Jones and I timed it once. That's why I liked Wink's name. It was quite short and easy to remember. He wasn't born with a last name at all, which was rather unusual. His name was just plain Wink.

Instead of crossing the point and going straight back home, we went the other way, towards town. We ended up walking along the wharf where the boats were kept, not far from downtown Bottlebay. The reason the town had that name was because a long time ago, there used to be lots of bottle factories here. There still is a faded advertisement painted on the side of an old brick building that says BOTTLED IN BOTTLEBAY.

Derek was frowning again, and even though he was much taller than me, I could still look up at him and see his eyebrows turning down, especially after we got into town. We passed some benches and clipped bushes and flower gardens. Derek looked a bit uneasy.

"I do like benches. They're quite nice, really," I said. "Shall we have a seat for a moment?" Even though Derek didn't want to, we found a very good one in the quiet park, and we sat down feeling dreadfully, weakly hungry.

Across the park and through the trees there was a school. Derek and I tried to look the other way, but it seemed to be pulling at us just like a magnet.

"There it is," said Derek, pointing across the park to the big brown school building. "That's where I'm *not* going this fall."

"Me either," I said. "It's very dark and menacing looking, isn't it." I stared at the large school building for a while. The name of the school was carved in stone above the door. It said THE JOHN E. BABBINGTON ELEMENTARY SCHOOL.

"Now, how did John E. Babbington get to have a school named after him?" I said. "I should like one day to have a school named after me. I should like very much to see one day 'The Felicity Bathburn Budwig Elementary School.' Wouldn't that be lovely? How do you suppose you arrange something like that?"

After a while, we got tired of sitting on the bench, swinging our feet and trying *not* to look at the John E. Babbington Elementary. Since we were both so very hungry, I was working away at Derek, trying to convince him to spend his quarter at the drugstore and soda fountain in town. I had always wanted to try an American soda fountain. Derek stalled a bit, kicking a stone about on the pavement, and I said, "Derek, nobody cares about your arm but you."

And finally, because of extreme hunger, he gave in. We crossed the street right away because neither one of us wanted to walk on the same side as the school. And all the way to the soda fountain, I sang "Good King Wenceslas" because of the footprints in that song and the way we had walked in Uncle Gideon's on the beach. And anyway, I do love Christmas carols.

When we got to Sal's, a drugstore and soda fountain, I went right in and sat on one of the stools that spin round. I could see Derek through the glass, standing outside, hesitating. I waved and smiled at him and I started spinning round and round. Then through the blur, I saw Derek push through the door and take the stool next to me. And soon enough, we were both spinning like tops.

Derek ordered a black cow. I did too, even though I

didn't know what it was. And I have to say, it was the best black cow I ever had, even though it was the *only* one I ever had. It was kind of a cold creamy chocolate drink with a lovely straw.

While he was sipping his black cow, Derek started working on the code again, writing out numbers on a napkin. And I looked in the mirror along the counter. There were mirrors everywhere in Sal's. They reflected into each other, and I could see a woman eating a tuna fish sandwich, repeated over and over and over again. Every time she took a bite, there were hundreds of her munching away, the same reflection going on into forever.

And Derek and I were there too. Flissy and Derek and Flissy and Derek and Flissy and Derek into eternity. It seemed to me then that I was ever so Flissy, and not much Felicity at all anymore. It was like I, Flissy, was on the shore, and Felicity was in a little rowboat, floating slowly away.

★ *Twenty-Eight* ★

The next morning, the telephone rang. The sound blaring through the house came as a complete shock to me. I honestly hadn't heard the telephone ring much before. I was lounging about in the parlor, reading *The Secret Garden* for the second time. (When I fancy a book, I like to read it at least five times. Uncle Gideon says I'm getting "obsessed" like Auntie Miami with *Romeo and Juliet*.)

The loud ringing almost caused me to fall off my chair, but only because I really like diving and falling and all that. It gets tiresome just sitting properly in a chair all the time. I think it makes things exciting once in a while to just fall over like you got struck by lightning or something.

Auntie was in the kitchen finishing up making more blueberry jam. Everything smelled of hot bubbling blueberries and steam. Uncle Gideon was up in the gymnasium, standing on his head. Soon enough, I heard a clunking sound, which must have been Uncle Gideon losing his balance and crashing over.

What I mean to say is, no one was able to answer the telephone but me. Anyway, I was the first to get to it, probably because I threw myself towards it, knocking Frances Hodgson Burnett's greatest work clear across the room. I slid in my stocking feet over the floor, bringing with me all sorts of cushions and newspapers and whatnot. Even though I am a proper British girl, I must confess that I grabbed the receiver. I was sure it was Winnie and Danny. They had always rung me up before. They would call and everything would be explained. And they'd have something wondrous for me...a new puzzle, a windup bird, a package of little paper umbrellas.

I picked up the heavy receiver and I was almost going to cry out, "Winnie and Danny, it's me, your Felicity! Where have you been? Where are you now? When are you coming home?"

But in the confusion and darkness of my head, I heard the voice on the other end, and it wasn't one I recognized. It wasn't warm and comforting. It wasn't Danny saying, "Hello, little think tank, miss you." It was a strange, brusque voice with an American accent.

"Hello, is this the Bathburn residence? Is Miami Bathburn there?"

"Miami?" I said, feeling then as if I had been a house made of bricks and had just been reduced to a pile of rubble by one of those whistle bombs.

"I believe so," I said quite politely.

"Well, we have good news for her. She has won the Bottlebay Women's Club raffle. The main prize being a twenty-minute slot in our upcoming talent and variety show. These twenty minutes are all hers. Rehearsal will start next week. May we speak with her, please?"

"Auntie Miami," I called out.

Auntie Miami came out of the kitchen, wearing an apron that was all covered with blueberry juice. The spots reminded me of blue teardrops falling across the fabric.

"Phone call for you," I said in a terribly casual way, going over to the curtains and looking up close at the stitching along the edges. And then I ran into the parlor and threw myself on the sofa. I grabbed a big straw sun hat belonging to The Gram and I pulled it down low over my ears and almost over my eyes. Then I fetched *The Secret Garden* from under a table and got behind it and started reading fiercely. Or pretending to read, anyway.

I sat there feeling very sorry indeed that I had done such a thing, that I had entered someone else's name in a raffle without asking that someone first. I hadn't really meant to do anything. Honestly, I never dreamed Auntie would win that raffle. I already had a sunburn, but I could feel my face turning red, red, even redder. Redder than Auntie's hands after steaming the blueberry jars. Redder than the poor jellyfish that I found on the beach last evening. He was all tangled up in seaweed, and you're not supposed to touch jellyfish, so I got a little pail and scooped him into it and took him back to the sea and let him loose in the water.

My face was definitely burning up. I pulled the hat down lower and I tried to read a passage from *The Secret Garden,* but words like *rose* and *rock wall* were sort of bouncing all about, and I couldn't get the words to line up and act like a regular sentence at all.

I tried to remember the moment I had written Miami's name on that piece of paper at the quilt sale. It seemed as if I had just arrived in Bottlebay. I did it for Mr. Churchill, didn't I? I didn't really know what I was doing. Was I sleepy? Yes, that was it. I had been terribly sleepy and mixed up.

I put my book down for a minute and listened. Winnie always said that British children should mind their own business, that they should not be nosy or impolite. I didn't mean to be nosy, but I could hear Miami very clearly. She was just saying, "Oh, oh, I see. Thank you so very much."

When she hung up the phone, she shouted out, "Felicity Budwig Bathburn, what have you done to me?" And she started crying and she ran upstairs to her room and slammed the door.

Uncle Gideon came down from the gymnasium, looking all interested, like someone was handing out free biscuits and perhaps it might be a good time to say hello. "What ho, Fliss," he said. "What's all the racket? What have you done now and where is Wink? Perhaps it's all his fault."

I held *The Secret Garden* up over my nose and I didn't answer.

"Sometimes I can be a good listener, Flissy," said Uncle Gideon. "Really."

"No," I said. "Thank you very much." I peeked at him over the book.

Finally, I broke down and said, "Wink didn't do anything. I did it all. I'm terribly sorry. But I did it for Prime Minister Churchill, actually. Yes, I did it for Winston."

★ Twenty-Nine ★

I decided then I absolutely had to disappear completely and forever. So I held the big hat down over my face and I pushed past Uncle Gideon and I headed for the upstairs. I tore down the hall, passing The Gram's room, hearing the buzzing of her sewing machine.

I planned to go up to my room to lock myself in forever. I was thinking Derek would have to design some sort of pulley system to send food up to me through the window because I was never going to answer the door, even if Derek came by and said, "Flissy, open up! I've got the code figured out." I was going to stay in there until I became a grown-up and then I would emerge, cool and calm, wearing high heels and red lipstick.

As I was running, I got the terrible feeling that I was about to cry. So I leaned against the wall outside The Gram's room. The feeling was coming towards me like one of the boats in the Cunard line, like the HMS *Queen Anne*, huge and gray and all painted over in her war costume, coming into the harbor silently. I knew it was going to happen.

I was truly sorry for what I had done to Aunt Miami. I hadn't even realized she would be angry or upset. Now all sorts of things were coming to a peak inside me. I could feel everything rolling towards me like floodwater.

I listened to the sound of the sewing machine. It was buzzing along as if nothing in the world was wrong, as if there wasn't a war across the ocean, as if my life hadn't been torn into a million pieces, as if Winnie and Danny hadn't left me here all alone in a strange land, not explaining anything.

The door was open a crack, and The Gram was sitting there sewing away, making something. She seemed to know I was out here in the hall all scrunched up in a heap about to cry. She turned round and waved to me. "Come over here, Flissy," she said. I waited. She waved at me again. Then I poked my head through the door very quietly. I could see the fabric she was sewing with. There were British flags printed all over the flannel. I went in to the room and stood by The Gram. And as I stood there, she smelled of roses and soap, and it was because of the soap and the smell of roses that I started to cry. If it hadn't been for the roses, it wouldn't have happened.

I cried and I cried and I cried and I laid my head on The Gram's soft shoulder and she hugged me and that made me cry even more.

"Go ahead and let loose," she said. "You've been very brave and you've been through a lot."

"I have?" I said.

"You have," she said.

"But Auntie Miami's angry with me and she'll never speak to me again. And you're angry with my Winnie. And when are they coming back for me? How long will I have to wait? And I know about Danny and Uncle Gideon. I know how they fought over my mum, Winnie. I know everything. The only thing I don't know is where my parents are and what they are doing. What are they doing?"

"Well, Danny has always been a terrible risk taker. You know that."

"Yes," I said.

"He's a risk taker and he wants to save the world. He won't be happy with less. Some people need the thrill of danger. But I'm angry with him and Winnie for hurting Gideon, and I have been for twelve years."

"Haven't Danny and Gideon started making up?" I asked.

"It seems that they have, or you wouldn't be here. In a way, you were part of the quarrel, though I am not at liberty to explain how," said The Gram, smoothing my hair away from my face.

"I'm not a part of their quarrel," I said. "I only just met Uncle Gideon when I came to Bottlebay. And were they really so close once?"

"Oh yes, they were the greatest of friends growing up. Though I will say Danny always seemed to outshine Gideon. He won all the games and races. Danny was so much more outgoing and better-looking than Gideon. Gideon was a bit in his shadow. But they were so close, they even spoke a secret language together."

"A secret language?" I said.

"Yes, and they went to the same university studying languages and they wanted to go into the same line of work. But of course, that didn't work out for Gideon. Still, in the end, Gideon has something that Danny doesn't have, and though I'm not at liberty to explain, that is what you call a blessing in disguise."

"And what about Auntie Miami," I said. "She's so

terribly hurt and angry with me." And I started to cry again.

"Oh, I think what you did was extraordinary. It was just what Miami needed. A good push. It was very forthright and clever of you. It must have been the Budwig in you that did it. We Bathburns are terribly, ridiculously hesitant and retiring. Except for Danny. Yes, it was the bold Budwig part of you that came up with it, and I think it is a grand idea."

"You do?" I said.

"I do," she said. "Now, let's put a barrette in your hair and pull it over to the side to show off your lovely Bathburn forehead."

"But the *Budwig* part of me wants to know something," I said. "When are my Winnie and Danny coming home?"

"Well, we can't know for sure, but we're going to wait. Waiting is hard, especially now at the edge of war. But we Bathburns are good at waiting, aren't we? Think about the sea captain's family that once lived here. They were Bathburns too, you know. How that family must have had to wait and wait and wait for their father's ship to come home. Imagine them rushing up to your room to watch the water for a sign. Finally, one day, perhaps they saw the mast of his boat slowly coming over the horizon."

"I hope so," I said. "And what are you making with this material covered with British flags?"

"Well, I'm making you a pair of pajamas, Flissy," said The Gram. "It will be getting cold soon and you'll be needing something comfy to keep you warm at night."

★ *Thirty* ★

It *was* already getting chilly at night. Somehow, summer was climbing towards an end, and the air had a different feel. I thought about all the times during the full summer that Derek and I had sat together at the top of the porch stairs, looking off at the horizon, as if an answer to the code might be found there. I thought about all the times we had stretched back on those steps, watching the sky turn over and change, as if every pattern above us might hold the answer to the letters.

But the light was different now and the ocean seemed gray again instead of turquoise. A bird's nest blew out of a tree in the garden that next day, and I brought it into the house, worrying about the babies. Gideon had said, "They're all grown and gone by now. Fall is here, Flissy. School starts tomorrow. Are you ready to get ready?"

I planned to give Auntie Miami the nest because she liked dried flowers and shells and things from nature, but she wouldn't answer her door when I knocked. I hadn't realized until then, when I stood there knocking away, that I had grown to love my aunt Miami. I missed our walks and our raspberry picking. She'd been in her room since the day before and I felt very sorry for it.

"Terribly dramatic, that one," said Gideon, rolling his eyes up towards her room as he passed me in the hallway earlier.

Today, Derek and I were supposed to get new shoes for school. The Gram had been a bit angry at Winnie about the shoes I wore here when she saw that I had a hole in the bottom of one of them. "But I *like* the hole," I had told her. "I can feel the ground a little bit and it's quite nice, really, to be able to know exactly what you are walking on." But The Gram didn't agree and she shook her head back and forth, looking at my shoe.

Now I was going to have to give up my ever so comfortable black English plimsolls with a nice hole in the bottom of one of them. I hadn't really outgrown them yet. But most of the other clothes I brought with me were getting too short and too tight. "You are growing in spurts, Flissy, and I think you've just had one of your growing sessions," The Gram had said to me a few days before. Uncle Gideon had taken a measurement on the wall near the kitchen when I first arrived, and when I stood against it recently, it was clear The Gram was right. I was getting taller. I wasn't nearly as tall as Derek yet, but I wanted to be. I stretched and stretched and hoped I could match his height. I thought it would be jolly nice to be tall enough to look straight across at Derek, face-to-face, without having to hop about and stretch my neck.

"Put on clean socks, Flissy," The Gram called up the stairs. "You can't try on new shoes without wearing clean white socks."

I was singing "Away in a Manger" and hoping Derek wasn't going to stay in his room forever this morning, though I had heard him calling out to The Gram that he didn't need new shoes because he wasn't going back to school. There were two Bathburns behind locked doors right now. Well, three if you counted Uncle Gideon in his secret study. So I decided it was really and truly a Bathburn trait.

The Gram had brought breakfast up on a tray earlier for Miami, and I had seen the tray sitting outside her door afterwards with everything all eaten up, and so at least I knew Aunt Miami was still alive in there. Then the Budwig part of me took hold again and I got out my writing paper and I began a letter to Aunt Miami.

Dearest Auntie Miami,
    I am ever, ever so sorry about entering your name in a raffle. The Gram says all you have is a

case of stage fright, which she says is completely
normal. But I would like to tell you it would be
lovely to see you onstage being Juliet finally. I
promise to go with you to every single rehearsal
and I promise to clap and cheer and laugh and cry
in all the right places. Please reconsider.

    Your adoring niece,
    Flissy B. Bathburn

After I finished the letter, I put on a new pair of socks and then I brushed my hair and I put the barrette back in. I peeked in the mirror to see how my Bathburn forehead looked today and then I gave Wink a wink and told him not to be antsy or fidgety while I was gone. I hadn't paid much attention to him recently. He was quite neglected now, but luckily, he was not at all aware of it.

I was just at the top of the stairs, when I heard The Gram calling out, "Derek dear, come now and let's get going. You can pick out your own shoes, whatever you like."

I slipped the letter to Auntie Miami under her door and then I went on down to the front porch. It was a crisp morning, and a slight feeling of cheerfulness was seeping through me. It had come through my toes and was up about as far as my knees even though Auntie was angry with me, even though Uncle Gideon was doing something secretive, even though The Gram didn't love my Winnie. Still, the cheerfulness was clearly at my knee-caps, even though most of the Bathburns were locked away pouting. But then I realized there were voices on the porch.

Voices? We hadn't had anyone here at the house before. Not a soul. It was not encouraged. Even when Derek had received a call from a friend in town, Uncle Gideon had written a note on a piece of paper and held it up while Derek was on the phone. The note had said, *"Not today. Not here, anyway."*

But now Uncle Gideon was sitting out there chatting with a man wearing a suit and a necktie. For some reason, seeing that made my new cheerfulness drain out of me. It dropped all the way down to my big toe and then sat there on the tip of it, ready to disappear entirely. Who was the man in the suit and why was he here?

The Gram called me into the kitchen. "Before we leave to go shopping, would you take this tray of tea out to the porch? There's a gentleman from Washington here to visit your uncle, and he wants to meet you."

"Me? Someone from Washington?" I said. "Does this

have something to do with my birthday being a day before the president's?"

"Not at all, Flissy, and don't forget the sugar," she said, putting it next to the teapot.

I took the tray out to the porch carefully and I set it down on the table. Then I stood there on one leg, trying to see what it felt like to be a blue heron. They stand on one leg all day in the marsh across the fields here. I was thinking about that, but I was also looking round at Uncle Gideon and the man from Washington. He had a briefcase with him, which appeared to have a little lock on it. I had never seen a briefcase with a lock before.

"Here's Winnie's daughter," said Uncle Gideon, nodding to the man.

"Ah," said the man, "I was hoping I would get a chance to meet you. Your mother is quite wonderful. Did you know that?"

"Where is she and what is she doing?" I said.

"This is Mr. Donovan, Fliss. It would be lovely if you'd shake his hand and say hello," said Uncle Gideon, beaming away.

"Hello," I said, switching legs and wondering how a blue heron kept from feeling tippy after a while. I shook

Mr. Donovan's large hand. Suddenly, my nose felt very itchy indeed. In fact, I felt itchy all over from my head to my toes and I just had to run upstairs and see Derek. It was of the utmost importance.

So I said, "Excuse me," in a very proper British way that would have pleased Winnie, and then I shot back into the house, as if I were a blue heron flying over the marsh towards the sea.

"Derek," I said, knocking on his door, "quick, let me in." And then I turned the doorknob and I rather barged in, in an American sort of way.

"Derek," I said, "get up quick. There's a gentleman from Washington downstairs. He's got a locked briefcase and he knows my mum, Winnie."

Derek was up in a flash, sitting with his legs crossed the way they sit round the bonfire at Camp Wabinaki, where he went for two weeks last summer. "Washington, DC?" he said.

"Yes, indeed," I said.

"Did he seem strange at all or unfriendly in any way? Is he questioning Gideon like an investigator perhaps?" he said.

"I'm not sure. You should go down and have a look at him," I said.

"Hmm," said Derek. Then he was quiet for a minute while I sat there feeling all fidgety, just exactly what I had told Wink this morning *not* to be. "That settles it. We have to get to Peace Island the next time Gideon goes there."

"I know," I said. "We're supposed to go buy shoes in town now, but on our way out, you must have a peek at Mr. Donovan before he gets away."

But when we got downstairs, Uncle Gideon and the man from Washington were no longer on the porch. And Derek was stuck. He had to go buy new shoes.

So The Gram drove Derek and me in the old Packard out through the rosebushes under the morning sky. The Gram managed to hit every pothole by mistake, and the wind seemed to push the car about like a little badminton birdie, and we sang "O Holy Night" over and over again because sometimes when I am worried, I sing. And besides, it was the prettiest Christmas song to sing in late August.

And so it was that Derek and I bought brand-new shoes for school. I got brown oxfords, which made me think of the school named Oxford where Danny and Gideon and Winnie had gone. And Derek got a pair of black canvas high-tops, which they call sneakers in

America and I teased him about them, saying he *was* a bit of a sneak.

And the whole time, Derek and I were in the shoe store with our feet being pinched and poked and measured, we were thinking about how we might find Mr. Henley and his boat.

★ Thirty-One ★

When we got back from town, Uncle Gideon and the man from Washington were still gone. But Wink was sitting on my pillow instead of by the window, where I'd left him. He was holding a white envelope in his paw or at least it was leaning against his paw. As soon as I saw that, I rushed up to him, snatching the envelope, leaving Wink looking rather stunned. (Perhaps he always looked rather stunned.) I couldn't help it. I was ever so curious, wondering who had written to me.

The outside of the envelope said, *"For Miss F. B. Bathburn, Care of W. P. Wink, Tower Room, Bottlebay."* In the back of my mind, I was hoping it was a letter from Winnie and Danny saying that the war was over and that they were coming back to get me. But then I felt a slight tug of regret, thinking that I wouldn't want to leave Derek all alone to face school without me. Well, perhaps if they were coming back for me, Derek could visit us in the summer.

I sat on the bed now and looked sideways at Wink. "Wink, tell me," I said in a half-joking sort of way, "who wrote the letter." I was thinking to myself, *I must truly be a nutter to be talking to a bear when I'm soon to be in the sixth form.*

There are two schools of thought about stuffed bears, Uncle Gideon said. It was true for adults who liked bears, as well as children. One theory is that stuffed bears know everything about the lives of humans they live with, the future and the past and the present, but they can't say anything. All they can do is give their love and support. The other school of thought is that bears know nothing at all about humans or their lives and they don't care a fig about any of it; they just offer unconditional love. That was what Uncle Gideon said. He could say things that were quite thoughtful sometimes and he often looked very "poetic," as Miami would say, when he was walking on the beach. And I did think it was a pity that he wouldn't play his piano anymore. I just couldn't quite decide what I thought about Uncle Gideon. And tomorrow he would become my sixth-form teacher, and I did hope he wouldn't tease me too terribly with all that British nonsense.

I knew, of course, it wasn't possible for Wink to answer me, and so I kissed his fuzzy ears and then I set about opening the envelope ever so carefully so as not to rip the paper at all.

When I got it open, it said,

Dear Flissy sweetest,

Of course I am not completely angry at you. I'm only a little bit angry because you didn't ask first about the raffle. But then I might have said no. And of course now I can't say no. So I'll have to say yes. Yes, I'll do it. But you must accompany me. And you must cheer constantly!

Love,

Aunt M.

P.S. Good luck with school tomorrow and see you at supper.

I put the letter down and went to the window. The ocean suddenly looked breezy and playful. The sky was all windy and blue, and Aunt Miami wasn't angry with me anymore.

Then I started thinking about what to wear tomorrow to the John E. Babbington Elementary. What did American girls wear to school anyway? In England, the girls wore dark blue wool skirts and a white blouse of your own choice. You had to go to a special department store for the blue wool skirts and dark blue knickers. Some richer girls had five skirts so they could get through the week nicely. I only had two and I lost one of mine once and I had to wear the same blue wool skirt for two weeks straight. But I didn't tell anybody. Then my other skirt was found under a pile of laundry. Thank goodness.

I opened my cupboard (or closet, as the Bathburns say) and began to look at my clothes. There wasn't much to choose from. I pulled out a cotton dress with little flowers all over it, but when I held it up, it was really too short. Then I noticed the yellow-checked suitcase at the bottom of my closet and I remembered the letter hidden under it from Winnie, written to Uncle Gideon. I remembered I was to wait till one week before Christmas to give it to him.

I got it out now and looked at the envelope again. It was all crinkled and wrinkled. I really wanted to open it, but I didn't. I stayed true blue to Winnie. But I thought over what The Gram had said about the fight and the blessing in disguise. I lay back on my bed, using Wink as a nice pillow (poor, patient Wink). I had two letters in my hands now. A letter from Auntie Miami in one hand and a letter from Winnie, unopened and unexplained, in the other hand.

Thirty-Two

And then it came, the day John E. Babbington had been waiting for. Knowing it was *the day*, I woke up early and I got right out of bed. I moved some things about, making a place against the wall. Then I stood on my head. I had been watching Uncle Gideon do it for three months now. I had been going into the gymnasium from time to time with a cup full of blueberries, and while he went to work getting his balance just right, I would look on and munch blueberries.

"It's good for the spirit, Flissy. And being all upside down is a super way to start the day," he said. "Everything just looks wonderful when it's all right side up later."

I hadn't told him, but I had actually been practicing a lot and I was getting used to standing on my head every morning just like Uncle Gideon. Not to say I liked my uncle, because I still thought he was a terrible teaser and possibly a great pretender, appearing to be nice when all along he was sneaking about snatching letters, keeping me from knowing where my parents were. And what about that poor piano? I was really quite dismayed and wasn't sure what I thought. I did very much enjoy learning to stand on my head. But what was it going to be like having him as a teacher?

As I clumped down the stairs in my new brown oxfords, I could hear a lot of bumping and banging and doors slamming. A typical Bathburn morning. Then Derek was sitting in the parlor, all dressed up in a nice pair of trousers and a blue ironed long-sleeved shirt. His hair was brushed back and it seemed to have Brylcreem in it.

Derek looked dashing and handsome and sweet and angry. Very, very angry. He was wearing that lovely sling that Aunt Miami had made for his bad arm. He didn't say a word. And neither of us fancied any part of any breakfast. As we were sitting there, *not* eating breakfast together, I wanted to reach out and take his hand in mine and hold it gently and say, "Oh, Derek. We'll see each other in the halls at school." But of course, I didn't dare; and besides, he was ever so grumpy this morning and he might have pulled his hand away and growled at me.

It was quite early in the morning, and after breakfast, I looked off the porch and saw that the tide was out, leaving all sorts of wet new things exposed, and there were whole chains of seaweed looping and stretching across the sand. I should have liked to run out to the edge of the world then, to find where the ocean had gone. I should have liked to have danced away on the long stretches of wet sand and to have slipped off over the horizon, but instead I had to go to school.

"What ho, Flissy and Derek! Two willing victims, I see," said Uncle Gideon.

Nobody answered him.

Derek and I went quite soberly to the car. Uncle Gideon drove along, humming a little song for a while.

"Who *is* Mr. Donovan?" I said suddenly, quite boldly in the silence of the car. Derek jumped up and started whistling loudly. Then he knocked the side of one of my brand-new oxfords with the toe of one of his brand-new sneakers.

"What?" I said to Derek.

Then Uncle Gideon said, "I do not want you to mention his visit at school, Flissy. It's, um, well, crucial that you don't, in fact. Can I trust you? Can I?"

"Well, then, who is he?" I said, staring straight ahead out the windscreen.

"He's a friend of an old buddy of mine from Dartmouth College."

"I thought you went to Oxford in England," I said.

"Oh, I did. But that was for graduate school. He's just a friend of a fellow I knew at Dartmouth. You see, that's all. Okay?"

I looked out the window and I tapped my foot on the floor of the car.

"Come on, Flissy. Forget about all that, okay?" Uncle Gideon said with one of those smiles that asked for a smile back. But I wouldn't. I never would. Even though he still loved my Winnie.

When we turned away from the ocean and headed towards town, Gideon looked over at Derek. Then he frowned and said softly, "Look here, Derek, why don't we say you broke your arm for now and leave it at that? No one will know the difference." Derek didn't answer either. He just kept looking out the window.

When we walked into the school yard full of American "kids," as they are called, Uncle Gideon put his arm across Derek's shoulder and his cheek on the top of Derek's head. "You can handle this, Derek. You can," he said.

Everyone seemed to rush towards us then to say hello to "Mr. Bathtub" and Derek and to look at me as if I were a creature from the moon, which I was wondering if perhaps I was.

British children are very brave and can often speak up when necessary. I told them right away in a very clear voice. I said, "My name is Felicity Bathburn Budwig and I am staying at the Bathburn residence while my parents are away on holiday."

And when everyone asked about Derek's arm, I told them. (I found out that day that British children in a pinch have a dreadful capacity to lie.) I said, "Derek fell down our fifty-two steps to the ocean. It was quite frightful. He tumbled like a rubber ball. I fainted when I saw it happen. It might have killed any other boy, but Derek only broke his left arm. They say it may take years to heal."

Then everyone looked very sorry for Derek, indeed. And they wanted to tell all about the time they broke a wrist or an arm. We had to listen to one little boy who went on and on and on about his brother and how he had broken his ankle while visiting the Catskills in upstate New York.

From everything I could gather, Uncle Gideon appeared to be quite popular with all the students and teachers. The librarian even called out to him in the hallway, "Mr. Bathtub, did you have a good summer?" The music teacher walked by, pulling a large black cello case and holding the chubby hand of a first grader. "Good morning, Mr. Bathtub!" she said, smiling.

Once we were installed in class, I had my own desk, and Uncle Gideon began calling me Felicity, which was ever so appreciated. He told the class we would be reading all the works of Frances Hodgson Burnett and then he said that I was an expert on Frances Hodgson Burnett, which made me feel quite lovely and very posh.

I looked round our classroom and I noticed there was a large photograph of Uncle Gideon all dressed up in a suit and bowler hat and sitting in an empty bathtub, reading a book. It said underneath the photograph, MR. BATHTUB SAYS, "READ." I did recognize the bowler hat, actually.

We had recess at ten o'clock and Mr. Bathtub told the class he was going home briefly and that he would be back in a flash just at the end of recess. I knew he was going home to get the mail. He didn't fool me. And when he came back, he was all out of breath and he looked quite somber and serious and he didn't make any more jokes until lunchtime.

★ *Thirty-Three* ★

I think the best part of going to school is when you're just leaving the building at the end of the day and the sun is shining and the rest of the afternoon is ahead of you. Then you just feel proud and not half chuffed because you didn't play sick and stay home.

I was waiting for Derek now outside the John E. Babbington Elementary School, which I learned today some teachers call the Babbington El for short. I hadn't had such a bad day, really, at the Babbington El. Mr. Bathtub had been rather lively in geography class, pretending to be the continent of Europe. He twisted himself all up and crouched under a table to show the state Europe was in right now with the war. Then later, he had us all line up outside and he blew his whistle, and everybody ran back and forth from one end of the playground to the other. Then he blew his whistle again and we all froze and dropped to the ground, which was ever so fun.

I met a girl named Rose, who was my desk mate, and I told her about Lily Jones and then I said, "I usually only make friends with people if they have a flower for a name."

I was just wondering how Derek had fared. Now as I saw him leaving the school, coming towards me, I thought he looked a bit glum. I still wondered all the time if there was any chance that Derek *liked* me. How did anyone find out such things?

"Gideon has meetings in the library," said Derek, "so we have to walk home."

"I see," I said, deciding *not* to ask him how his day had gone. "Hmmm. Guess who went home at recess to check the mail today."

"We really ought to talk to Mr. Henley," said Derek.

"Why don't we write him a letter," I said. "And since we don't know his address, we'll pop round and deliver it to the post office right now."

And so we did. We sat on the grass in the park across from the Babbington El. Derek ripped a page out of his notebook and wrote while I dictated the letter.

I said, "Dearest Mr. Henley."

And then Derek said, "I don't think we should address him as 'dearest' since we barely know him."

"Very well," I said, "Dear Mr. Henley, Derek and I are working on a secret project. We are observing the peculiar habits of the great blue heron."

"Are they peculiar?" said Derek.

"I don't know, actually," I said, "but it makes it sound more interesting, don't you think?"

"Perhaps," said Derek. "Go on."

"Derek and I will be writing a very complicated report, indeed. Could you, by any chance, give us a ride in your boat to Peace Island on a Saturday? I would telephone you in advance to let you know what time and which Saturday. Very truly yours, Flissy and Derek. P.S. I was terribly sorry to hear that you do not have a wife. Perhaps the following year will prove more fortunate."

And then Derek said, "I think we should cross out the part about the wife."

And so I said, "Oh, all right, then."

We folded the letter up nicely. (I had to help. That's another thing you can't do with just one hand.) Derek drew a knight on the outside, but he didn't put him on a horse because horses are too hard to draw and we were in a hurry.

Then we went off to the post office. We went up to the counter and I said, "Excuse me, is Mr. Henley here?" I could actually see him at the back, sorting mail. I saw stacks and stacks of letters and I wondered if any of Winnie and Danny's letters were in those piles. I could see how easily a letter could get lost or damaged. And what if a mail plane got shot down? Wouldn't all the letters then fall into the sea?

Soon enough, someone brought out a note from Mr. Henley. It said, *"Hi, I'd be pleased to give you a ride on a Saturday. I can check my lobster traps while you are on the island. Give me a call when you want to go. Bob."*

"Oh," I said, once we were out on the street again, "Mr. Henley's name is Bob. Bob Henley. How lovely."

I saw for a moment that Derek was kind of laughing. His laughter was always a rarity. As rare as a yellow sea finch, if there is such a thing. As rare as a sea turtle in a tide pool. Oh, I did so want to put my arms round Derek just then and lean my face against his. But of course I didn't, because British children are ever so proper. Mostly.

★ *Thirty-Four* ★

Derek and I were going to have to wait for the right Saturday to phone Mr. Henley, and that wasn't going to be easy because we didn't always know exactly *where* Uncle Gideon was. Last week, the music teacher and the art teacher from Babbington El were walking along the beach. They were both wearing straw sun hats even though it was late in the season. They called out and waved to me, "Hello, Felicity. Is Mr. Bathtub around?"

"No," I called back. "I don't know where he is." And I didn't.

Rehearsals at the town hall were to begin that week in the evenings and I had to make good on my promise to Aunt Miami. And you can always count on a British girl to know how to knit and to know how to keep a promise. About six o'clock just after supper, when it was time to leave, I started looking for Aunt Miami.

In the kitchen, Uncle Gideon was finally doing his turn washing dishes, making a big display of it, I thought. "You see, Fliss," he said, holding up a Brillo pad, "the other day when you said you'd *never* seen me wash a dish was a complete exaggeration." And then just to make his point more dramatic, he put on one of The Gram's big aprons, threw a dish towel over his shoulder, rubbed his hands together, and began singing "I've Been Working on the Railroad."

I do love that song so very much and I wanted to join in, but instead I stood there with my arms crossed, waiting to see if he was actually going to wash a dish or two. Soon enough, he had all the soapy teacups stacked up high and he called them The Leaning Tower of Teacups. "Want to help me, Flissy? I could use a good assistant," he said. But I hurried off without turning round. He always looked a bit blue when I wouldn't join in with one of his awkward projects. I had to get upstairs to see what was keeping Auntie Miami.

When I went into her room, Auntie Miami was sitting at her dressing table. She was brushing her hair and staring sadly at herself in the mirror the way people do when they are only half sad and they find that sadness fascinating to watch.

"I'm all ready to go, Auntie," I said. "I've got my shoes tied and my jacket all buttoned, and The Gram braided my hair." And I spun in a circle so that my braids flew out behind me. "The Gram says now I look all tidy and properly taken care of. I told her I've *always* been properly taken care of. And The Gram said, 'No, I really think Winifred was too busy to care for you properly.' And then I said, 'That's not so. Winnie always brushed my hair.' Are you ready to go, Auntie?"

I sat on the edge of the bed and remembered Winnie brushing my hair, back in London. We were playing beauty parlor. Winnie's hair was so fine and light and her skin was pale and she wore dark lipstick.

"Winnie is very beautiful," I said to Aunt Miami. "The Gram forgot to say that. Are you almost ready? Shouldn't we be leaving?"

Auntie Miami looked down.

"You are going, aren't you?" I said.

She didn't answer. She kept looking at the lovely little things on her dressing table.

"Auntie, you *have* to go. They are expecting you. You are a great actress. Winnie always told me when you are called to do something, when you have greatness in you, it is bigger than you, it's beyond you, and it is your duty to follow it through. That's what Winnie says."

Aunt Miami smiled at herself in the mirror. Then suddenly, she turned round and got up and put on her sweater with beads along the collar. She took my hand,

and as we walked towards the stairs, she looked at me and said, "Flissy B. Bathburn, you are a strange little duck, you know that?"

And I leaned my head against her arm and I looked up at her and smiled and I said, "Quack. Quack."

Thirty-Five

By the time we got to the first rehearsal, we were quite
wet as it was raining that night. It was a real autumn
rain, the kind that, when you hear it, you know summer is definitely over. Yes, summer was over. The
ocean was saying it as it rushed again and again against
the rocks. The wet trees were saying it as the wind
pulled them back and forth, shaking loose orange leaves
that blew over the road. The dark, rainy sky was saying
it too, all the way to Bottlebay in the old sneezing,
freezing Packard.

And the windows wouldn't roll up. The handles just
went round and round and did nothing at all. Before we
left, The Gram had brought out a couple of blankets to
put over us, and Uncle Gideon had waved his arms about
and directed us out of the driveway. (He was still wearing that silly apron.) He leaned in the car window and
looked quietly at Aunt Miami. "Take good care," he said,
patting the top of the car. Then he wanted Derek to
go along in case we needed help with backing up and

directions. Soon Derek came running through the rain in his macintosh and wellies, and it was jolly nice to have him in the backseat, offering advice to Auntie Miami as she drove along in the windy, rainy darkness.

Yes, we were ever so wet when we got there. So wet that we made a rather gloomy puddle under us as we stood in the town hall. Mrs. Boxman, who was the director of the program, came flying towards us with a thermos of tea swinging from her hand and she poured us three cups and we stood there warming up while she congratulated Aunt Miami on winning the raffle.

There were all sorts of people sitting on the stage waiting with fiddles and flutes and drums, and there was a yodeler wearing a Swiss costume, just like you'd see on tins of powdered cocoa. Mrs. Boxman said, "Florence, *you* are to start the program. You will be first as the winner of the raffle. What are you going to perform?"

Miami looked rather sweet and wet standing in a puddle of water. "I'd like to do several scenes from *Romeo and Juliet*." Auntie smiled.

"What a marvelous idea," Mrs. Boxman said. "We'll have costumes, props, the works. It will be a smash hit. Who will be your Romeo?"

And suddenly, Miami went silent and blank like a photo that had just come shooting out of a photo booth completely empty with no image on it at all. "I hadn't thought about it," said Aunt Miami, and it looked to me like she might start to cry. She turned away and stared down at her hands.

That's when I panicked. My eyes rolled round the room from one person to another. Then they stopped and there was Derek in his handsome macintosh and wellies, looking so tall and so sweet. To me, at that moment, he was the most perfect Romeo in all the world, even wet as he was. And I called out, "Derek. Derek will be Romeo."

"Oh," said Mrs. Boxman, "of course. Well, he's young, but he's tall and bonnie, as they say in England. I knew you'd have everything worked out, Florence dear. After all, you are Danny's sister. And Danny was once my student and wasn't he a wonder! Oh, I just thought the world of him. How is he doing and where is he, by the way?"

"He's away on holiday," I said, and then for a moment, I felt like a ship, like the SS *Athenia* drifting along at sea, hearing the sound of a submarine churning nearby.

Then I noticed Derek was looking rather muddled and confused and gruff; his hair was messed up and he looked rather like a bull pawing the ground, thinking about charging. "Romeo? Me?" he said.

I went round and stood by him and I whispered, "Please, Derek. Just for now. Please. Just to get her started. Just for practice until we can find a real Romeo."

★ Thirty-Six ★

I always thought I was properly cared for. My hair was always brushed, and Winnie always made sure my skirts were hemmed. I had all my manners. I was sure of that. But it's true there were nights when I was alone. I never liked waiting by the window after dark, watching for Winnie's white wool jacket under the streetlight, watching for Danny's overcoat and scarf and his felt hat. They often came up the walk late. Ever so late. I never knew what they were doing or where they went or why.

Once right before Christmas, there was a phone call, and Winnie and Danny had to go away. Winnie cried about it. It's strange to have someone else's tears on your cheeks. She hugged me and cried and said, "Oh, I'm so sorry, darling. So terribly sorry. Will you forgive me ever? Danny and I have to go. It's terribly important. Alice will be in to get you. You'll have Christmas with her and her father. We'll celebrate afterwards. Later. It will be lovely." Her tears dried on my cheeks by the time Alice Wentley, our housekeeper, arrived. Winnie and Danny had already left. I was glad to hear Alice's footsteps on the stairs. I thought she'd never get there. We left our flat and our Christmas tree all decorated with unopened presents sitting under it. I hoped that no bomb would fall on our flat while we were gone. I did so want to open my presents.

I went to the country with Alice in a car. We didn't say much the whole way there, except that I sang Christmas carols without stopping, one after another, without catching my breath in between. Across the city, I could see all kinds of bombed-up buildings and fires burning. "You really shouldn't be in London anymore at all," said Alice.

"I know," I said, "but Danny works there."

"Well, we're lucky we had some petrol in the tank. Just about enough to get home. And that will be it. They'll have to come out for you when they get back."

"We are going to have our Christmas when Winnie and Danny come home in two weeks," I said, and then I started right in with "Once in Royal David's City" and I didn't stop singing till we were past a huge pile of bricks partly covering the road. Those bricks had once been a building, and bunches of bobbies (policemen) in capes were waving us by and blowing whistles.

When we got to our housekeeper Alice Wentley's cottage, she said, "Well, now, here we are at Hollyhock Hill.

It's got a registered name, our house does. And it's where I live with my father, who's feeling poorly these days."

I carried Wink, who seemed quite miserable, into the little brick house, and Alice called out, "Daddy, we're here. We barely made it. Would you like a cup of tea?" They had a tiny Christmas tree on the kitchen table, but it wasn't real. It was fake. I could tell when I touched it. "Lucky we had that in the attic or we wouldn't have had a tree at all, would we. I don't know where your mother found your Christmas tree in London with these times being as they are."

"She found it in Piccadilly Circus. A man was selling some. It was ever so dear," I said.

"Well, Daddy, here's Felicity Bathburn Budwig come for Christmas with us. What do you say, Daddy?" Her father was lying on the sofa in the small parlor, under a blanket. I didn't know if he could turn his head or not since he always stared at the ceiling. "Daddy, say hello, won't you." It was strange to hear a very old woman, Alice Wentley, calling an even older man Daddy. Because I'd never called Winnie and Danny that sort of thing. Everybody thought it very funny at first. Winnie said I was terribly grown up in some ways and terribly childish in others.

Alice Wentley's father said, "How old is she?"

And I said, "I'm ten years old, though I'll be eleven in January." But he had already started coughing and didn't even hear the part about my being eleven soon. He didn't say much after that except, now and again, he would call out, "That chap Churchill is a bloody fool."

Christmas Eve was a few days later. Alice Wentley cooked Christmas pudding, and her father spit it up. That night I lay awake in my bed in the tiny room near the kitchen. I was thinking about Winnie and what she had said that night before they left. She said, "Felicity, it's so hard. I have a kind of calling. It's my work. My work is important to me, but *you* are also important to me. I'm torn between those two things. Don't you see? I'm torn in two."

All Christmas Eve, I lay in bed looking up at the ceiling like Alice Wentley's father. I was listening for bombers in the sky. They said there would be a cease-fire that night in London for Christmas, and I was hoping it would be true.

Thirty-Seven

Even though Uncle Gideon had said to forget about him, the man from Washington bothered me. Why had he come here to Bottlebay, Maine, and how did he know my Winnie? Even if Derek and I didn't talk about the code all the time, it seemed to be always with us or near us like the sound of the ocean. We thought of it especially at rehearsals when Aunt Miami and Derek were repeating those lines that we hoped held the answer. Derek often looked at me as he said his lines, but then I was never sure what he was thinking. Did he know I liked him? It nagged at me. Was it possible for an older boy to like a younger girl?

"You know, Flissy," said Derek one day after school, "I can't keep playing that Romeo part. I hate doing it, you know. I only did it this far just for Miami because it is nice she's getting to be Juliet finally. But honestly, Fliss, I hate it."

"You do such a lovely job of it, though," I said. "But of course we'll find someone else." We were sitting on the porch swing pushing it in circles in a lazy sort of way. It was almost October and there was a smell of smoke in the air. The leaves fell from the tree next to our house all at once that afternoon, filling the sky with fluttering yellow light. The summer people had all gone home, and most of the beach houses down the way were shuttered and boarded up.

"Anyway, those lines are stuck in my head now," said Derek.

"I know them by heart," I said.

"Tell me something, Flissy. When you saw the book of *Romeo and Juliet* in the locked study that day you went in there, was it open to those very lines?"

"I think so," I said. "But I can't be sure because I was in such a hurry. *Something* was circled with a pencil."

"And how many letters do you think we've gotten, all together?"

"I think there are six, though we haven't received any for over a month." And just as I said that, I began to have a sort of anxious feeling that started to hover over me like a dark overcoat hanging above me in a closet.

"You know, Fliss, we need to go back into the study and copy over the other letters and look at the book of *Romeo and Juliet* that you saw in there."

"I see," I said. "I suppose you're right."

"Flissy," he said, "let's go down to the side yard and look up at the house from below."

And so we did. From down in the south yard, the house seemed enormous and tall, with great, crisp-looking autumn clouds sailing slowly beyond the roof. "Have a look at the windows on the second floor. Count them. The one that is the third from the end is the study. The other two are part of the gymnasium," said Derek.

"Yes, I think you're right," I said.

"And there's a screen in the window today. The window's open." A few yellow leaves floated in the air. "I'll need a ladder," Derek said. He pushed his hair off his forehead. I closed my eyes. He wasn't afraid at all.

"It's a great thing that no one is home right now. When is Mr. Bathtub due back?" I said.

"He usually stays at least an hour after school," said Derek. I was following him down the slope that led under the porch, where the basement door was. We pulled the long ladder out of the darkness and carried it up to the side of the house and set it against the wall.

It was an oddly quiet afternoon. Even the ocean seemed hushed. Shadows were velvety and muffled, lying across the house. "Derek," I said as he climbed the ladder and I held it steady at the bottom, "be careful. Do. And by the way, can I have the little broken tin soldier. Please?"

"You mean if I don't make it back alive?" Derek said, looking down at me quite sweetly. The ladder swayed and I held on tight.

To keep from being nervous, which is my way, really, I closed my eyes and wrote another letter to Winnie and Danny in my head.

Dear Winnie and Danny,

After having discovered Derek Bathburn Blakely here in the house at Bottlebay, I am afraid to say that I have rather fallen for him, though I don't want to use that word "fallen" just now, as he is up on a very high ladder and it's a bit rickety.

More later, I hope, if we don't die doing this.

Love,

Your Felicity, who is most definitely a nutter

Derek had climbed all the way up the ladder by then. He was just at the window and he was leaning against it, reaching for the screen, which meant he wasn't holding on to anything because his other arm could do nothing but hang at his side. I watched him pull the screen out of the window with one hand. Derek always amazed me. Then he lost his balance, with the screen swinging around in the air. Finally, he dropped it, and it went spinning and sailing down, bumping against the ladder. It landed with a flat thump in the sandy grass near where I was standing. Everything else was silent.

"Oh, Derek," I whispered, "be careful."

Luckily, the old peeling window stuck open and Derek inched up on the ledge and was able to duck his head inside and then slip the rest of him off the window ledge, down into the room. Then he shut the window.

And so I was left below gripping the ladder, shadows from clouds above drifting in a soundless way across the house. "Derek," I whispered again. "Derek? Derek?"

I couldn't wait. I wasn't sure if it was the British part of me or the antsy Budwig part, but I began to climb the ladder in a shaky sort of way. A group of ring-billed gulls overhead were screeching as they landed on the roof above, breaking up the silence in the air. When you are climbing up high, it is probably a good idea not to turn round and look behind you. And so I didn't. I just kept climbing and watching the road in the distance for a sign of the black Packard and Uncle Gideon or a cloud of dust that might mean a car coming along. When I got to the top of the ladder, I held on to one of the shutters and I pounded on the window.

Derek looked at me through the glass. "Go back, Flissy, it's not safe," he mouthed. But I stayed there pushing against the glass. I daresay I didn't generally take orders very well. Danny often said I would not make a good soldier.

"No," I shouted. I held up the screen I was carrying. It flew about in my hand like a gull caught in a draft. Derek rolled his eyes. He opened the window and I climbed partway in, huffing and puffing, dropping the screen into the room. Half of me was in and half of me was out, and Derek was pulling on part of me while another part of me had one of my dreadful laughing attacks. And then suddenly, I fell in on the floor. I lay on my back with my arms out trying to imagine what it would feel like to die. Did you float to the ceiling when it happened?

"Were you worried about me terribly, Derek?" I whispered, still breathless. "Would you cry at all if I had died?"

"Flissy," Derek said. And he then didn't finish his sentence. He looked a bit stunned.

"What?" I said.

"Here's the box you saw delivered a while ago. It's open."

"What's in there?" I said, getting up quickly and going over to look at the box. Derek reached in and pulled out a small crocheted pincushion with an embroidered butterfly across the front.

"Is that all?" I said as I looked at the box and the postmark I had grown to know so well. "May I hold it?" With the pincushion in my hands, I had a fleeting image of Winnie sitting by candlelight, her embroidery needle darting quickly over some fabric.

"We should put it back," said Derek, reaching for it. But just then, he noticed a small two-inch opening along one seam. "Well, I see something was tucked *inside* here," he said, "but it's gone now. Someone has removed it." He stared down at the floor.

Then he started opening drawers in the desk where the letters had been before. The drawers as he slid them out squeaked and dragged in the soundless air. Finally, he pulled out a stack of letters, all six that Gideon had received. He held them up towards the light.

We spread each letter out on the desk. It was really startling to see them all lying there. We slipped them gently from their slit envelopes. Each letter was full of a series of numbers and nothing else. We copied them over as quickly as possible.

"Anyone on the road?" said Derek, looking up at me. I ran to the window.

"So far no, but hurry," I said. "Have we got every letter copied?"

Derek nodded.

Then we went through the envelopes, quickly checking the postmark dates. Yes, it was true. I was right. We had not had a letter for a whole month. I put my face in my hands and looked at the blackness behind my closed eyes. Why had the letters stopped coming?

"It's getting late. Come on, Flissy," said Derek. "You leave by the study door. I'll lock it behind you."

"But what about you? Poor you?" I said, pulling a little on his shirtsleeve.

"Quick, go now," said Derek. "I hear a car up on the road. Go. Now."

★ Thirty-Eight ★

"What ho, Fliss," Uncle Gideon called as he got out of the old Packard. I stood off to the right of the house so my uncle would look towards me and not off to the left, where through the rosebushes he might glimpse the edge of an old tall ladder and a clever boy climbing down it. Uncle Gideon had a briefcase in one hand and a pile of papers in the other. There were books in his arms too, and it looked as if he might drop them all at any second.

"Lovely day, isn't it!" I called out, hopping about on one foot. I always seemed to do that when I was nervous. "It hasn't rained at all. Not even two drops." And I changed to my other leg and started hopping again.

"Yes, it is a lovely day, a quiet day," said Uncle Gideon, looking at me sideways and frowning. "You are hopping awfully well these days. Are you in training for a hopscotch tournament?"

"No, no, I'm just rehearsing something. Um, thinking about rehearsing. I mean practicing something. I mean hopping is good for thinking, isn't it."

"Ah, I see. That makes sense, I think. Well, since we're on the subject of rehearsals, how has my sister been doing at the town hall?"

"Oh, she has been doing a topping good job," I said.

"Did you say a whopping good job?" he asked.

"No," I said, "a topping good job."

"And she's not dropping out, is she?" he said.

"No, she loves being Juliet," I said trying to think of other things to keep the conversation going. "Yes, she really does."

"Yes or no?" said Uncle Gideon. "Which what?"

"Well, I'm not sure. She loves it, that's all."

"Oh, she's a hopeless romantic," said Uncle Gideon. "I guess we all are around here."

"Probably not me," I said.

"Well, then you'll be the first Bathburn that isn't, Flissy."

"Why does everyone love *Romeo and Juliet* so much when it's such a sad story, really?" I said, nodding my head up and down to make sure Uncle Gideon looked my way.

"They love it because they can see themselves in it," Uncle Gideon said, and then he turned his face up towards the sky. A formation of airplanes was flying overhead in a V shape like geese heading south for the winter. If only they were just geese.

"Bad news every day with the war," he said. "But your England is putting up a good fight."

"What will happen if we lose?" I said.

He shook his head. "By the way, Fliss, you haven't collected the mail for me and forgotten to give me anything, have you? I mean like a letter or anything?"

"No, I haven't forgotten," I said.

"I mean, the mail is usually on the dining room table when I get home from school. I mean, you didn't see a letter for me?"

"No, I haven't seen one," I said, and then my heart got heavy again and fell like one of those black-crowned night herons dropping into the sea to feed.

Just then, a gust of wind whipped round the house the way it does sometimes even on quiet days and it ripped all the papers from Uncle Gideon's arms and it swirled them all over the garden like a group of autumn leaves. Some of them flew about and landed in the rosebushes off towards the left. I ran after those, and Uncle Gideon chased the ones along the front of the house. I could see now that Derek had finally moved the ladder. I took a deep breath.

When I had grabbed all the papers on my side, I happened to see (quite by accident, honestly) my report on Frances Hodgson Burnett. Mr. Bathtub had written *A-plus* at the top in red and added, *"You are a marvel! Well done, Felicity Bathburn! You truly are an expert on this delightful author."*

I felt rather guilty and sorry indeed then that Derek and I had broken into the locked study and poked about in his desk while Uncle Gideon had been off correcting papers cheerily, writing nice things on the top of my report.

"Good catch, by the way," he said, taking the papers. "We wouldn't want to have a whole swarm of sixth-grade reports flying about in Bottlebay, would we? Some of the spelling errors would shock the general population!" He smiled a little bit and then he started heading towards the house. Soon he turned round for a moment and said, "I say, old bean, beautiful report you wrote. By the way, I've noticed your math is a bit off. You know, we can fix that."

"Thank you, Mr. Bathtub," I said, looking up at him, feeling worried and guilty and mixed up and sorry for him suddenly for loving my Winnie and having to sit alone in the dark, listening to sad songs, missing her.

Thirty-Nine

The rehearsals at the town hall were going very well. We went almost every evening during the week. Aunt Miami floated quietly around the room, but when she stepped out onstage, it really did seem to become all hers. Derek learned the lines, but hardly tried. He was always looking off stage as if he were just about to walk out and leave the whole thing. And he was constantly saying, "Fliss, help. Find someone. Do something. I hate this."

Still, whenever he was onstage, I thought he was wonderful, and I knew I loved him all the way down to my bones.

At rehearsals, I usually sat next to Mrs. Marlene Fudge, who had a trained parrot with her in a cage. She was hoping one of the acts would step down so there would be room for her and her singing parrot. I often chatted with her. I even asked her once if her name was really Mrs. Fudge. "Yes, I married into the Fudge family," she said. "And they are not a very sweet bunch at all, I can assure you of that."

Sometimes just to be winning, she brought in a plate of fudge for everyone in the cast. She was so hoping someone would cancel, which is why I kept begging Derek not to drop out. Not yet, anyway.

And besides, he was so smashing onstage. I wished, as he said his lines so halfheartedly, I wished that I was his Juliet and that he was my Romeo. I would gladly have thrown myself on the floor and died while giving a long, tearful speech onstage, if it would have meant that Derek would kiss my cheek.

I thought perhaps that Derek was the first boy I ever loved. And then I remembered Michael Hardy in first form. He happened also to be in my very small Sunday school class in London. We always held hands in Sunday school and it was our great secret because in regular school, we never even spoke to each other.

And then there was a little boy named Charlie in third form. Once, we were standing in a queue for lunch and someone said, "Oooh, you like Charlie Snappet? *He* has false teeth." And Charlie said, "I do. Want to see them?" And he pulled out his two front teeth and held them in his hand. But it didn't bother me because when you love someone, *nothing* they do bothers you.

When rehearsals were over for the night, and Derek and I were sitting on a bench outside, waiting for Miami, Derek said, "I've been looking at all six letters, and every time Miami says her speech, I try to think how those numbers and that speech might be connected."

"I forgot to notice, Derek, when we were in the study. Did you see the copy of *Romeo and Juliet*?"

"Yes, it was there," he said. "And we were right. Miami's favorite lines were circled in pencil. Flissy?"

"Yes?" I said very hopefully. I liked being in the dark with Derek.

"I had to take out the trash this morning," he said.

"Oh, poor Captain Derek," I said. "I promise I won't tell your soldiers."

"And when I poured the trash into the barrel, I saw this," he said and he held up a tiny metal film canister. He lifted the lid off with his thumb. The canister was empty.

"That's nice," I said, "but it's rather small."

"Well, it's plain and it wouldn't mean anything to anyone else, but it might mean something *to us*."

"What?" I said.

"Well, why would someone throw out an empty film canister?"

"Because they didn't need it anymore," I said.

"Yes, because they gave the film to someone else. Perhaps. And the film must have been about two inches tall and this little canister, when it held the film, might fit perfectly inside a little pincushion," said Derek, looking up at a cluster of gray night clouds drifting towards the horizon.

★ *Forty* ★

Most of October went by and Uncle Gideon did not take his walk down the beach with the folder under his arm, headed for Peace Island. He didn't go that Saturday or the next or the next. And so we didn't call Mr. Henley. We just waited, and Derek got a book out of the library about codes and code breaking and he would read parts aloud to me once in a while. But the book was terribly complicated and wasn't much help.

We were given homework at school, and Mr. Bathtub wanted everyone in our class to read the newspaper, so I went into the library in the late afternoon and I sat at the oak table in there and looked at the headlines again. I read that Nazi tanks called panzers had gone all the way to Moscow and it was looking as if Russia was losing to the Germans. I read that a Nazi officer named Fritz Holtz had been killed by the French Resistance in a town called Nantes in France and that the Nazis had then killed fifty hostages to pay the Resistance back. I read that Nazi submarines continued to torpedo boats crossing the Atlantic. I read that they even came in close to the shores in America and prowled about as I had suspected. And then I put the newspaper down and felt sad and shivery and I looked out the window at the choppy October ocean.

And then another week passed and it was almost Halloween, my first. Derek and I planned our costumes and worked on them. Derek decided to go as Sir Gawain. He made his entire suit of armor out of cardboard and glitter and glue. He even made a helmet with a movable face guard.

I wanted to go as Frances Hodgson Burnett. Aunt Miami said she would help me with my costume. She went up into the attic with me and we opened old trunks, looking for the perfect Victorian dress and hat. Auntie kept finding things for the play and Juliet, like a lovely red velvet cape with a fur-trimmed hood.

As I was trying on a long white cotton dress with lace all over it and a bustle at the back, Aunt Miami said, "You know, Flissy, you really are growing up. It seems as if it is happening right before our eyes."

"Do you think anyone will know I am Frances Hodgson Burnett?" I asked.

"Well, you can carry *The Secret Garden* around," said Aunt Miami. "And hold it up when they ask. Because they always do ask. They never figure out anything. You could be a ghost in a sheet with two holes for eyes and they'd still say, 'And what are you dressed up as, dear?'"

And then I said, "May I ask you a question, Auntie?"

"You'd better not, Flissy. The Bathburns tend to prefer silence."

"Auntie, why did The Gram decide to adopt Derek? What made her do it?"

"Oh, perhaps to cheer Gideon up," she said, closing the trunk. "Remember I told you he was heartbroken when he came back home to Maine. He had lost everything. But anyway, you shouldn't be asking all this, and I didn't even know you knew about Derek. You're going to get me in trouble, Flissy Miss. Let's just not talk about it, shall we?"

"Oh, look," I said, "there's a parasol and it's only a little bit ripped. May I use it for tomorrow? Pretty please?" Miami trailed away and our conversation broke off as usual, and it wasn't finished until late Halloween night.

Derek and I were all set to go trick-or-treating that night, but as we walked out along the beach, Sir Gawain and Frances Hodgson Burnett, every house was shuttered up and dark. We kept hoping one might be lit. But they were all gloomy and hollow and casting windy shadows in the early moonlight. Now the Bathburns really were the only family on this point and we came back with our sacks empty.

We had to drive into town to the church basement where they were having a Halloween party. Uncle Gideon took us and when he got out of the car, he put on his yearly costume, a big papier-mâché bathtub that went round his waist. He was carrying a long-handled bath brush, and now and again he would scratch his back with it and sing, "Scrub-a-dub-dub, three men in a tub."

And he was ever so pleased with my costume. "May I have your autograph?" he said when I got out of the car. "Oh my, now I see. It's you, Flissy. Well, you fooled me completely. I thought Frances Hodgson Burnett had finally come to Bottlebay, Maine."

"Remember she died in 1924," I said, trying to shut the rusty Packard door.

"Just give it a swift kick," said Derek.

"Excellent advice, Sir Gawain," Uncle Gideon said tapping his long-handled bathtub brush against Derek's sparkly sword.

I was thinking about Miami and how she came out in the darkness as we were leaving earlier. She had pulled Mr. Bathtub aside and whispered, "Gideon, they called from the Halloween committee and asked for someone to play the piano at the party tonight. Would you do it this once?"

"No," he said quite loudly. His voice seemed to growl, and he stood up tall for a moment like a great bear in Yellowstone Park. I had seen photos of those grizzlies in the *National Geographic* magazine in the library.

At the party, we played a game called bobbing for apples. Derek bit five apples that were floating in a tub of water while his hands were tied behind his back and he had almost fifteen cents in his pocket when we went home. All I had was a great bib of water on the front of Frances Hodgson Burnett's lovely white dress. But I also had two small waxed-paper bags full of candy corn, peanuts, and popcorn balls because we had stopped at a few houses in town to trick-or-treat. One of the houses belonged to Mrs. Boxman. "Oh tra la la!" she said when she opened the door and saw us. "It's Romeo himself!"

Derek frowned and closed his face guard down and said through the cardboard, "I'm not Romeo, I'm Sir Gawain."

When we got home, The Gram and Aunt Miami were playing hearts in the parlor. I went into the dining room, looking to see if any letters were on the table.

There were none. In the library was a newspaper, a few days old, dated, October 28, 1941. I read, "Yesterday on Navy Day President Roosevelt gave an inspiring speech, trying to convince all Americans that the Nazis pose a dangerous threat to the entire world."

I sat under a lamp in the library in my Frances Hodgson Burnett dress. The wind sighed like a ghost at the window, and I heard Miami scream out. It seemed to shatter the house. The Gram had just beaten her at hearts again. Soon she came rushing into the library.

"I hate that game, especially with just two people." Miami said. "I'm never playing it again." She sat down on the piano bench and put her elbows on the nailed-down lid.

"Auntie," I said, "what are you doing? Uncle Gideon said not to touch the piano."

"Oh, I never listen to *him*," she said. "Anyway, he's gone upstairs."

"Tell me, Auntie," I whispered, "tell me *now* why he has nailed the piano shut. Why?"

"You never give up, do you? You are like a little spotted sandpiper on the beach, those little birds that never stop running up and down. My poor brother. He is *so* talented. And handsome, really, in his own way. I have to tell you the music teacher at Babbington thinks he's wonderful. You know what I mean."

"I see," I said. "And the piano?"

"Yes, well, okay, but you mustn't say anything. In England, Gideon had a part-time job as the jazz pianist in a club at Oxford while he was finishing up school. Danny had been away writing his thesis in France and he came into the club that night and met Winnie for the first time. Gideon was at the piano supplying the lovely music. Danny talked with Winnie for a while and then he asked her to dance. You know the rest of the story."

"Was it not very nice of my Danny?" I said.

"No, it wasn't," said Miami, "but it was romantic, wasn't it? When Gideon came back home to Maine, he nailed the piano shut, and he has never played another note since then."

★ *Forty-One* ★

I will be twelve years old in three months, which makes me eleven and three-fourths. I have been in Bottlebay now for six months, since May, and in those six months, I think I have grown five inches. Derek said I was a mere pipsqueak when he first saw me, and it feels like ages since I had a birthday.

We were still in London when I turned eleven. I thought, because of the war, I wouldn't have a proper birthday, but Winnie had been saving a secret stash of sugar and flour and she made a little birthday cake for me. She woke me up singing "Happy Birthday" and brought me the cake with a candle burning on it while I was still half asleep.

When I got up, we made short work of that cake and it was a lovely one too. Winnie knew how to make little blue roses out of icing and she put them round the edge of the cake. "In another life," she always said, "I will be a baker and I will have a shop full of beautiful rose-covered cakes."

Danny was smiling at her with great admiration, but at the same time, he looked a bit sad. There is a photograph back in London in our flat that shows Winnie and Danny and me with the lovely birthday cake. Alice Wentley took the picture. She said it was the last time she would come in to London. And that's when Danny said, "Oh, we'll be leaving soon anyway." And he put one arm round Winnie and the other round me and smiled. Alice Wentley took another photograph.

Then Winnie said, "Go get one of my hats and put it on and we'll do a birthday photograph of you wearing a big birthday hat." And so I did. I went into their bedroom and looked about and then I opened the cupboard door and started rummaging a bit, looking for a hat, which I found.

And while I was in the cupboard, I saw a man's overcoat hanging there in the darkness. I hadn't noticed it before. And when I opened the front of the coat, I saw it had a French label. For some reason, that made me look in the inner pocket. Then I pulled my hand back quickly because there was a gun in there. It was small but different from a toy gun in that it was very heavy, and when I let go of it, it dropped back down deep into the pocket.

I went on to sing another round of "Happy Birthday" with Winnie and Danny and Alice Wentley in the kitchen, and later when I thought about it, I tried to remember what I had really seen and I wondered if perhaps it had just been a dream.

★ Forty-Two ★

That autumn in Maine, the USS *Denobola* arrived in Casco Bay. We read about it in the Portland papers. It was a great big tanker that was sent here to service the whole fleet of US destroyers that would leave from Portland harbor to escort the cargo ships crossing the ocean to bring supplies to England. President Roosevelt had decided finally to protect and accompany the cargo ships with American destroyers because the Nazis had been sinking hundreds of cargo vessels as they crossed the ocean. They were trying to cut off the food and fuel supply to England.

Sometimes we could see a fleet passing along the horizon, one cargo ship with a group of big US destroyers surrounding her. Derek and I loved to watch them through our binoculars. Uncle Gideon too would come out on the porch and stand there with us, waving to them. He said without those cargo ships, England would starve.

Derek said that he had seen the cruiser ship the USS *Augusta* going by with seven destroyers protecting her in August. That was the ship that was supposed to have been carrying President Roosevelt back from his secret meeting with Mr. Winston Churchill. Derek said the ship he saw was flying a blue flag with four stars, which meant there was an admiral on board. At the time, he didn't know that President Roosevelt might also have been on board. A few days later, Roosevelt was spotted in Rockland, Maine, and that's when everyone figured it out. Still, no one knew where the secret meeting had taken place. Oh, I wish I had seen the USS *Augusta* go by that day, but I was out in the salt marsh with Auntie Miami sketching.

For that whole autumn, Derek and I kept on waiting for Uncle Gideon to go back with his folder to Peace Island. But so far, he hadn't gone at all. Both he and I continued to wait for a letter from Europe, but no letter came, and Uncle Gideon seemed quieter than usual and more than once he stopped me on the porch or in the kitchen to ask if I hadn't seen a letter or misplaced a letter. I always had to say no.

One Saturday after breakfast, the mail was delivered by the weekend postman, an older gentleman who moved quite slowly and sometimes mixed up the mail and gave us letters belonging to the White Whale Inn down the beach. I fetched the mail that day and there was nothing much there, just a newspaper or two. I could see Uncle Gideon looking out through the lace curtains in the dining room, watching, waiting. After that, he seemed rather cross, which was not his usual way at all. Then, just about midmorning, all of a sudden he set off down the beach anyway, with his folder under his arm. He didn't walk as briskly as he had earlier and he seemed to be looking for an answer in the sand beneath his feet.

★ Forty-Three ★

Derek and I rang up Mr. Henley immediately. Thank goodness he had a telephone as a lot of people along the coast did not. It was a brooding windy day actually, not exactly rainy, but the sky was almost without color. A lot of the trees above the shore no longer had leaves, or if they did, they were raggedy and wind-torn and brown.

When we reached Mr. Henley on the telephone, he told us he would like to check his lobster traps and that it would be good to get out on the water. We were to meet him at the dock in front of the White Whale Inn, which was way down the beach to the north of our house.

The White Whale Inn was closed now since the season was over, and all the windows and doors were boarded and shuttered up like everything else out here, but the dock was still in use. Derek and I arrived early at the dock, and while we were waiting, I looked up at the large weatherworn inn. It seemed completely deserted. I quite hoped that Mr. Churchill and Mr. Roosevelt had come here for their secret meeting in August, when the hotel had been open. I tried to imagine them sitting out there in wicker chairs talking about the war. "Do you think they came here for their secret meeting?" I called to Derek.

"No, silly!" he shouted back. "They went up to Newfoundland. Everyone knows that now."

"Still, it would have been the perfect place, don't you think?" I cried out into the roar of the ocean. "And it would have been lovely to have them so near by."

Just then, we saw Mr. Henley's small lobster boat coming round the bend and we ran down to the dock and waved. And when he came up and shut off his motor, we climbed in. Derek put a life jacket on me. He tucked it right over my head and showed me where to buckle it, and all the while, I was looking into his face and thinking that he was ever so knowledgeable.

Mr. Henley asked right away about our secret report on the great blue heron. "But aren't they gone by now, migrated south, or do they stay behind all winter?" he said, starting up the motor again.

I stared blankly at Mr. Henley. "Um, well, actually, great blue herons decide at the last minute.... Um, that's why they stand on one leg; they are deciding about migrating. Should we go or should we stay? That sort of thing."

"Our secret report will cover all that," said Derek, nudging me with his good elbow.

The boat was cutting through the water now and I was looking down into the depths of the ocean for seals. In the summer, you often saw them sunning on rocks. We putted along through the waves, the shore and rocky cliffs passing by above us. We saw the Bathburn house then from a distance with its widow's walk and the tower room at the top of the sky. The whole place seemed wrapped in isolated autumn silence.

Derek said, "I heard there was some waiter at the White Whale Inn this summer who took off during his shift and cut all the telephone wires to the inn."

"He was unstable," said Mr. Henley. "He just up and left. No one knows where he went. I guess the police were looking for him because the guy had a bunch of Nazi flags in his room."

"And they say we are teetering on the brink of war," said Derek.

"Yes, they do say that," said Mr. Henley. "Any day now, I'm guessing. Any day now.

"A sea so gray I woke all night
and rose at dawn to find dark light.

"Like poetry?"

"Usually," I said. "You seem very different to me without your postman's suit on. I almost didn't recognize you. You look like a true fisherman."

"Ah," said Mr. Henley. " '*All the world's a stage and all men and women merely players. They have their exits and their entrances and one man in his time plays many parts.*' William Shakespeare, a great poet and a true visionary."

"Mr. William Shakespeare?" I said. "Isn't that the chap who wrote the play *Romeo and Juliet?*"

"Indeed it is. The greatest playwright ever."

"Shakespeare?" Derek said. "Would you say that you enjoy his plays?"

"I would," said Mr. Henley. "I'm not just a mailman and a fisherman. I also write and read poetry. I send my poems to the *Saturday Evening Post*, hoping to get published. But they always send them back to me, saying 'No, thank you. No, thank you. No, thank you.' "

"Well, it's their loss, Mr. Henley, I'm sure," I said.

"Yes," he said.

"So," I added, "did I hear you say you favor this Mr. Shakespeare?"

"Yes, I most certainly do," said Mr. Henley. "As

a reader and a writer, I most certainly favor Shakespeare."

Derek and I looked at each other straight on. Our eyes snapped tight and we both nearly jumped up out of the boat and leaped into the tossing sky.

But we were nearing Peace Island. It loomed before us, and thousands of birds, whole clouds of them, were calling and crying and fluttering against the rocky cliffs that seemed to jut straight up from the sea.

Forty-Four

I followed Derek as he climbed the steep path that zig-zagged up the side of Peace Island. There were wild, scruffy, autumn-colored rosebushes on either side of the narrow way. I could look straight down and see the now-green deep water far below us. Seabirds like puffins and storm petrels and terns and seagulls hovered and landed on the cliffs above us. I could see Mr. Henley and his small blue lobster boat moving out towards the open sea. I rather wished he would have stayed closer by.

The wind was picking up. It was almost howling, like a choir singing in Saint Paul's Cathedral in London. I kept hearing The Gram in my mind saying, *Stay off those rocky bluffs to the south of here, Flissy. The wind gets ferocious over there and a little stick of a girl like you could be swept out to sea in a snap.*

When we had climbed all the way to the top of the cliff, where the island then flattened out into long waving grass, we could look off into the distance and see Mr. Henley's boat getting smaller and smaller.

"Romeo, Romeo, wherefore art thou Romeo?" I called out to the wind.

And Derek said, "Shhh. We're not alone on the island, remember. But you're right, he *is* our Romeo. Why didn't we ask him outright, Flissy? We should have."

"No," I said, "we can't risk it. If we ask him outright, he might say, 'Oh no, I'm way too busy.' We really must be terribly clever about this. Don't you think?"

I looked off one more time at the sea stretching away into forever. Mr. Henley's boat was fast becoming a blue speck on the horizon. What if he forgot to come back for us? What if a stray Nazi U-boat prowling about the coast came upon Mr. Henley's little lobster boat?

Seabirds still circled overhead, and the long switch grass rolled and rippled and simmered like water. "Come on," said Derek. "Hurry. We don't know how long Gideon will be out here. Let's head to Savage Point."

"Savage Point?" I said.

"Yep, it's named after a hermit who used to live out there. He took care of the lighthouse. His name was Joe Savage. People in town used to say, 'Joe Savage took a bath once a year, even when he didn't need one.'" Derek smiled up and out at all that was before us.

"There's a lighthouse?" I said.

"It's not in use anymore since they built a new one over on Turtleback Island. The Savage Point Lighthouse is pretty much abandoned."

The wind was behind us and it felt as if we blew through the wide field of grass, as if we were flying across the open stretch, as if the clouds were piling up higher and higher above us, as if the dark trees against the sky were ripping back and forth faster and faster. Derek got ahead of me and I had to call out to him to slow down, but my voice seemed lost in the wind. Finally, we came to a wooded sheltered area and we slid down a steep slope into a rocky, bushy glen and then we went through a group of trees that were short and bent over, as if they had been standing up too long against the weather.

Just on the other side of the trees, there it was, the Savage Point Lighthouse, sitting high up on the farthest and outermost spot on the island, the final piece of land before the vast open Atlantic. We came upon it slowly although the wind seemed almost to push us along. The lighthouse was gray, a forlorn bitter gray. Its windows were broken. The door hung open on loosened hinges. A rope was strung across the path and

there was a sign hung on it that said DANGER. NO
TRESPASSING.

As we got closer, we began to hear a noise like a small
motorboat coming from inside the lighthouse. I looked
out at the ocean and could see nothing but the endless
water, with no sign of Mr. Henley.

Derek stepped over the rope and moved towards the
half-open door. He took my hand in his and suddenly,
though I was scared, my hand felt tingly and warm lying
in Derek's hand, almost as if I could feel all of Derek's
being in his palm pressed close to my palm. I followed
him through the door, nothing between our palms, just
his against mine.

Inside, light came down in shafts through broken
windows from above. Old plaster lay on the steps that
curved round and up, round and up, to the top of the
lighthouse. Palm against palm, I followed Derek. The
noise was a kind of even hum now. Up the steps and
round the first turn, we looked out a broken window
straight down into a drop-off to the sea below. Round the
next curve, there was more plaster, an old pair of boots
set off to the side, a bird nest above a broken window, hay
and bird droppings, and the low drone of a motor as we
rounded up and up. Then at the top there was a green
wooden door mostly closed, only a crack left open.

Derek, still holding my hand, leaned closer and we both peered through the crack. Uncle Gideon was sitting at a table, his back to us. On the table was a machine connected by a wire to a small motor on the floor. Uncle Gideon was tapping out something on the machine. Even over the motor, we could hear tap, tap, tap. Tap, tap, tap.

★ Forty-Five ★

Everything sifted through me that next week like a great confusing kaleidoscope—the image of Uncle Gideon sitting at that table with his back to us, the man from Washington who had visited with the locked briefcase, the film hidden in the little pincushion, the gun in the overcoat pocket in London, the calling away of my Winnie and Danny, the Romeo and Juliet code, and the letters. The letters. All of it seemed to fit together to form a picture that felt blurry and dark to me, a picture I couldn't quite read. All the images cut and fluttered and changed form in my mind at night. Then the house would seem even darker and more ominous. There were shadows on the stairs. Lights seemed to flicker in the parlor. The news of the war on the radio would play in my mind over and over again.

And yet, by day, everything seemed to go on as usual. No one seemed worried that the Nazis might come here in their U-boats. People were not ordered to put dark curtains over their windows at night to keep the light from alerting planes overhead of our presence. There were no food rations, and most anything you needed you could buy in the grocery store in downtown Bottlebay.

"Flissy, of course you would be more sensitive to all that," said Aunt Miami. "You were there and saw all of it." We were sitting in the library. The whole Bathburn family was in there reading away. Uncle Gideon got up for a moment to put on some water for tea, and when he returned, we both suddenly looked at Aunt Miami. She was back behind her book, reading again. Uncle Gideon and I happened to see the cover of the book both at the same time, and it was not *Romeo and Juliet.* Aunt Miami was reading a book called *The Great Gatsby* by F. Scott Fitzgerald. I looked at Uncle Gideon and he looked at me. Then he put his hands together like he was praying and he rolled his eyes up at the ceiling and smiled. Aunt Miami had broken free.

It was mid-November, and Thanksgiving was soon to be here. I had never had a real American Thanksgiving before. We did actually have a little mock Thanksgiving in London once, but after dinner, Danny looked a bit disappointed.

"Never mind, darling," said Winnie, patting Danny on the back, "we'll have a real Thanksgiving in

Bottlebay, Maine, one day soon, with all of your family, perhaps after the war when all our differences can be patched."

Naturally, I was looking forward to Thanksgiving. At school, Mr. Bathtub had us all drawing turkeys and cutting them out and pasting them in the windows. He said it was a Babbington El tradition. There were turkeys in all the halls and cutouts of pilgrims' hats with buckles on them pasted up everywhere and it was all jolly good fun. No one seemed very worried about U-boats snooping about in the harbor.

Mr. Bathtub told our class that President Franklin Roosevelt had recently changed the date of Thanksgiving. He had moved it to the third Thursday in November instead of the fourth Thursday. He did that because America was not doing very well financially and he thought that it might boost Christmas sales to have a slightly longer time for people to buy things after Thanksgiving and before Christmas. This year, we would be celebrating Thanksgiving on the twentieth of November instead of the twenty-seventh.

"A lot of people do not like the change in holiday," said Mr. Bathtub. "They call the holiday Franksgiving and have made an uproar about it. But in our house, the Bathburns of Bottlebay will be celebrating on the

twentieth with President Roosevelt." And the class
cheered.

That week, I decided to write President Roosevelt a
letter. I went up to my room, smiled quickly at Wink,
and set to work. I did notice again that recently I hadn't
spent much time with Wink, which would have been
quite sad except that Wink was clearly changing and
hardly seemed dependent on me anymore. I got out my
paper and wrote in my best British penmanship:

Dear President Roosevelt,

*I am a British girl living in Maine for the
duration of the war. I should like you to know that
I am a very big fan of yours. So is Derek, who is
also a polio victim like yourself. My grandmother
has been to Warm Springs, Georgia, and says you
help children with polio in your spa there. Derek is
quite wonderful and was adopted at age one. I
actually hope some day to marry him. (That fact
should remain in your secret files!!!) Anyway, I'm
looking forward to Franksgiving. Keep up the
good work and please say hello to my fellow coun-
tryman, Mr. Winston Churchill.*

Sincerely yours,

Felicity Bathburn Budwig, age 11

*P.S. Thank you ever so much for your help
escorting cargo ships to England with all those
fine American destroyers.*

I brought the letter with me on the way to rehearsals, which sometimes took place after school. Across the front of the envelope I had written, *"To: President Franklin Delano Roosevelt, The White House, Washington, DC, USA."* I was ever so pleased to be able to post a letter really and truly, since so many that I had written to Winnie and Danny were simply piling up in a box under my bed, more and more of them every day.

★ *Forty-Six* ★

We had extra rehearsals that week and they were becoming quite difficult. Derek stopped being willing to play Romeo at all and didn't show up one day, which put Mrs. Boxman in a frantic mood and caused her to ask Mr. Fudge, when he stopped by with his wife, if he might read the part for the evening. And then Mrs. Boxman found a spot in the lineup for Mrs. Fudge and her singing parrot. I thought she did a very good job and I was glad that parrot finally got his chance.

Mr. Fudge, however, proved to be a dreadful Romeo. "He killed every line," said Aunt Miami to me on the way home that evening.

All this made me decide that Derek and I *had* to figure out a way to get Mr. Henley to the town hall right away. And so the next day, as we were leaving school, I said to Derek, "I think we should visit Mr. Henley at the post office this afternoon."

"Good idea, Flissy," said Derek. "And?"

"We'll tell him that Mrs. Boxman has two free lobster traps to give him over at the town hall. Well, she

does, Derek. There are those two extra lobster traps
that they couldn't use in a scene last night, and Mrs.
Boxman asked if anyone wanted them and no one did,
so they're still there on the stage. And then we'll ask
Mr. Henley to hand-deliver a letter to Mrs. Boxman
while he's there. We'll say we don't have an address
and we don't have time to post it. We'll ask if he could
pop round this evening at six thirty and give her the
letter and pick up the lobster traps."

"That *will* get him there for sure," said Derek. "Flissy,
I think you're a genius. What will the letter say?"

"Hmm," I said. "It will come to me. You write it
down." And we sat on our favorite bench outside the
John E. Babbington Elementary, Derek with pen in
hand and me with my eyes closed, tilting my head back
towards the sky. I began:

Dear Mrs. Boxman,

*Mr. Bob Henley, who is standing before you, is
an expert on William Shakespeare. I believe he
favors him entirely. He is also a poet and a reader
and will make a simply grand Romeo. Perhaps
you should ask him now.*

Sincerely yours, Fliss and Derek

P.S. Mr. Henley will like the lobster traps as well, I should imagine.

And we *were* able to entice Mr. Henley to come round to rehearsals that evening. Of course it was the lobster traps that did it. He used them to catch lobsters, but he also collected old and interesting ones, and it is generally known that collectors will go anywhere to find yet another addition to their collection. I had heard that Mr. Henley's cottage was all decorated with lobster traps hanging from the ceiling and nestled among fishing nets above his fireplace. And someone said he calls his house Henley's Haven.

About six thirty, Mr. Henley had come promptly through the double doors at the town hall looking all-business and brisk and still in his postman's uniform. He handed the letter to Mrs. Boxman and then began inspecting the lobster traps that Derek and I had set out in plain view.

Mr. Henley explained to me how the lobster comes into the kitchen area of the trap, tempted by the food that lures him in. Mr. Henley waved his arms in the air, mimicking the lobster.

"Then, when the lobster tries to get out, he goes into

the parlor, where he becomes hopelessly trapped," said Mr. Henley.

As Mr. Henley pointed out the kitchen and the parlor of the lobster trap, Mrs. Boxman was reading the letter. He was just testing the parlor door on one of the traps when Mrs. Boxman, who had just finished the letter, said, "Tra la la, Bob, we're in a bit of a pickle here. We're down a man in one of our acts. We desperately need a Romeo for our performance coming up at Christmas. I heard you like Shakespeare and I *know* you like poetry. Would you consider taking on the part of Romeo? We mostly rehearse in the evenings after work."

Everyone in the room seemed to gather round Mr. Henley quietly. There was a long silence. I thought of a group of seals in the ocean circling one lone big fish. Mr. Henley continued looking over the second lobster trap, turning it this way and that, saying nothing.

Finally, he looked up at Mrs. Boxman. His face was like the sky at dawn, luminous, light-filled, joyous, and slightly pink. "Indeed I do love Shakespeare and I would be honored and pleased to accept the part in *Romeo and Juliet.*"

Everyone in the room started clapping. Mr. Henley basked in the applause. "Thank you. Thank you," he said. "And yes, I do write poetry, and in fact, I happen to have a poem I wrote, here in my pocket. May I read to you?" And so he did. But the poem went on a bit too long and when he brought out a second one, Mrs. Boxman suggested they get started with rehearsals.

While they were rehearsing, Derek and I went outside and kicked a stone about on the sidewalk. We could hear Aunt Miami calling out onstage, "O Romeo, Romeo, wherefore art thou Romeo?" We stood there in the darkness together looking at the big, glowing Bottlebay moon and thinking quietly of the code we could not crack.

★ Forty-Seven ★

After rehearsals, I did end up "musing," as Uncle Gideon says, about the story of Romeo and Juliet. Romeo and Juliet were two people who loved each other so very much. Because of their families, they were not supposed to be together, but their love was too strong to ignore or deny. Perhaps that was how it was with Winnie and Danny. Even though Winnie had been married to Uncle Gideon for a short time, when Winnie met Danny, their love for each other was something so special that they had to follow it. It must have cost them greatly, but I was ever so glad they did or I wouldn't have been born and wouldn't have been here at all.

Yes, Romeo and Juliet were a bit like Winnie and Danny. But wasn't Gideon too a kind of Romeo, even if his Juliet had found another? I was musing about all this as I rolled out pie dough with Aunt Miami on the morning of Thanksgiving. Every time I dusted the pastry board, I thought about Romeo and Juliet and all the ways they truly reminded me of Winnie and

Danny. Lily Jones told me one day that she thought my parents were like two stars. "Very glamorous-looking, the both of them," she had said as we were paging through one of her movie magazines.

We had been expecting enough relatives for Thanksgiving that we had made place cards for the table. I had made the place card for Cousin Brie, a girl just Derek's age. "You've never had a real Thanksgiving, Flissy?" said Derek earlier. "I love it because of the turkey and because my favorite cousin, Brie, comes over after dinner for pie. And she's pretty."

"Oh, how very *nice*," I said, trying to not to make that word *nice* sound prickly like a spiny sea urchin. But somehow it came out prickly anyway, because none of my words ever did what I wanted them to. But in the end, the arrival of Cousin Brie turned out actually to be another blessing in disguise.

I heard that phrase over and over again through the year. That's what Danny had said of my having to go live in America with his family. "It'll be a blessing in disguise. She'll love it. I did. No, really, it will be like giving her a great gift. The best gift we could ever give her." Winnie had cried and cried and then Danny had put his arms round her.

Yes, Cousin Brie did turn out to be a full-blown blessing in disguise. A terrible one. She and her mum showed up after we'd had Thanksgiving dinner. We were just serving the pies we'd made. Mine looked rather sorrowful because I had forgotten about it in the oven and it was a bit singed. But it was still quite edible. Uncle Gideon had two pieces and he kept saying over and over again, "Flissy, you've done it again. This pie has a marvelous smoky flavor. I'll have another!"

Cousin Brie pointed to my pie and said right away, "Ooh, who made that pathetic-looking thing?" But already I had misgivings about her anyway, because in England, Brie is a kind of stinky French cheese.

After dessert, Derek and Brie and I went off to the parlor alone. We could hear all the relatives talking in the next room. Brie told us that she was wearing brand-new expensive saddle shoes that came all the way from Marshall Field's in Chicago. Then she said, "Cousin Derek, where did the little creep with the snooty accent come from?"

I did think that her saddle shoes were ever so lovely. They had a blue saddle on them instead of brown or black, and the laces were twists of many colors.

She was much taller than me, about the same height as Derek, and they stood back to back to see if either of them had grown taller than the other since they'd seen each other last. I had to get up on a chair and put a book over both their heads to see if it was level, meaning they were still the same height. And they were. Then they patted each other on the back like they were club members after a special meeting.

"Does the little creep have a real name?" said Cousin Brie, dropping back down on the sofa and putting her feet up on the low table in front of her so she could look at her saddle shoes. "I mean other than Fleecy or Flossy or whatever. And how long is she going to be here?"

And Derek said, "Maybe forever."

And Cousin Brie said, "Oh, swell."

Being British, I tried to pretend that I hadn't heard her at all. Then I thought of Danny. When I used to be sad when we were down in the tube in London, all crowded in, waiting for the bombers to pass, Danny would look over at me, and just with his sweet Danny eyes, he could make me feel better. He could say just with his eyes, "Love you, little think tank."

Cousin Brie was a dreadful thing. She usually rode horses with Derek when she came here because there was a stable a mile down the beach on the other side of the White Whale Inn. But today, Derek said he couldn't go riding with her because it was Thanksgiving.

"Too bad you hurt your arm," she said, retying her shoelaces. "Will it be better by next week?"

Derek said, "Oh, maybe."

We ended up playing Parcheesi at the card table by the window. The whole game, Brie kept sending my green people back to the beginning and pushing her red people farther along and trying to sit ever so close to Derek. They laughed a lot and he told her all about Sir Gawain.

"Go ahead, your turn, L.C.," she said to me. L.C. was short for Little Creep. I kept thinking how Derek had said I might be here forever.

And then Derek got on the subject of codes and secret messages and I was afraid Uncle Gideon might pop his head in the door and say, "What are you talking about, old thing?" But he didn't, thank goodness. The grown-ups were all too busy in the kitchen arguing about President Roosevelt and Mr. Winston Churchill and the Far Eastern situation.

"Codes," said Brie. "All I can say is, when Mother was little, she used to play with Uncle Gideon and Uncle Danny and they always sent messages in code to each other."

"Yes?" said Derek.

"Yes," said Cousin Brie. She went on to say that her mother told her the best way to do that was for both people to decide on a passage from a book beforehand. But you don't tell anyone the name of the book or what the passage is. Then you write numbers in order from one to two hundred above each letter in the passage. "That's your key," she said. "When you go to write a note, you use the numbers above each letter instead of the letters. It works." Cousin Brie rolled the dice and made a blockade with two of her red people on the Parcheesi board. "It's impossible to crack if you don't know which passage is being used. And you're blocked, Derek. You lose a turn. What do you say?"

But Derek didn't answer. He just looked at me and nodded his head up and down. I felt shivery all over like I might call out or cry or jump up and down, but I hoped it didn't show. I felt like tossing myself in the air or kissing Derek on the cheek or squeezing Wink. But that was the least likely to happen because Wink was all the way upstairs, and besides, once I had turned eleven, I had learned it was better not to hug a bear in public.

Something about the Bathburns and hearts and Parcheesi, they never lost. Derek's purple men rallied and came up from behind like knights on horses and began to win. Just steps away from the final defeat of the stupid red people, Cousin Brie knocked over the Parcheesi board, saying, "Geez, sorry, I was just trying to tie my shoe."

Her mum called from the hall, "Brie love, we should be going now." Then the awful, terrible, dreadful Cousin Brie flipped her hair about and stepped up and kissed Derek good-bye. He looked rather sheepish and blushed as red as one of the Parcheesi pieces from the red team. Then Brie looked at me and said, "See you later, L.C."

And her mum said, "L.C. Is that your new nickname, dear?"

And Cousin Brie said, "It stands for Little Cutie." And she gave me a fake smile.

Everybody, except for Derek and me, went out on the porch to look at the sunset. We heard Uncle Gideon say, "Well, we are going to be getting into the war any day now. Should have done it sooner. I don't know what we are waiting for." And everybody went down the steps towards the beach.

I was running round the room like a piping plover or a laughing gull, diving back and forth in front of the fireplace. Derek was lying on the sofa, looking up at the ceiling, "Thank you, Cousin Brie. Wasn't she wonderful! Wasn't she super? We've got it now, Flissy. I can barely wait until they leave. She did it. She did it. She gave us the key." He sat up. "We have to go try it as soon as their car is out of the driveway."

And so we took Juliet's speech and the copy of the first letter and we went all the way to my tower room. The moon had come out again and it was even more huge and yellow this time, floating above the ocean. I always loved now to see the moon because I soon realized it was the very same moon that hung over England every night. All countries share the same moon. It hung over England every night whether bombs fell or not, whether sirens screamed or not. The moon was always there.

We got the Juliet speech out and we sat on my bed and Derek wrote the numbers over each letter in each word so the speech looked like this:

1 2 3 4 5 6   7 8 9 10 11   12 13 14 15 16 17 18 19 20   21 22 23
O ROMEO, ROMEO, WHEREFORE ART

24 25 26 27 28 29 30 31 32
THOU ROMEO?

33 34 35 36 37 38 39 40 41 42 43 44 45 46 47 48 49 50 51 52 53 54
DENY THY FATHER AND REFUSE

55 56 57 58 59 60 61
THY NAME,

62 63   64 65 66 67 68 69 70 71 72 73 74 75 76   77 78   79 80 81
OR, IF THOU WILT NOT, BE BUT

82 83 84 85 86   87 88   89 90 91 92
SWORN MY LOVE,

93 94 95 96 97 98   99 100   101 102 103 104 105 106 107 108 109   110 111 112 113 114 115 116
AND I'LL NO LONGER BE A CAPULET.

And the Par Avion message looked like this.

12-5 21-2-10 64-35 17-7-41-47-110-14. 52-47-46-77-72-16 23-1
80-53-20 70-71-15-5-72-31-53-82. 33-64-2-115-110-81-96-29-86
40-71-86-33-64-99-104 48-115-91-96-110-105-82 25-59-91-54
101-29-110-109-55-50-95 4-18-53-73 100-40 37-43-78-30.
59-98-82-29 80-99-K-58-84-70-47 48-1-80-77-89-108
46-104-14-35-81 96-103 19-111-74-K-53. 89-44-37-116-16-15-82
66-1 57-75-80 91-71-111 110-8-80-19-64-50-63 59-47-48
104-113-64-33-14-82 81-84 112-83-2-42-52-104-41-72 46-53
82-93-65-108 111-98-66-54-15-99-21-55-96-91-61.
79-80-23-116-78-63-51-89-39 82-10-76-37-96-94-104 80-112
110-11-99-81-41-110-116-82 21-103-48 82-41-65-31
25-90-80-53-44-82 96-58 114-57-6-99-53. 79-5-109-45
25-21-82 53-10-55 113-112 1-51-40-96-110-92 37-90
40-93-89-82-64-51-88 112-109-112-14-85-53 111-74-33 112-98-21-99
5-82-110-109-112-44 85-3-52-24-16-53. 77 21-74-48 107
70-71-89-114 107-20 81-93-K-71-58-104 65-100-80-2
110-25-71-101-33-15-115-58 24-3 53-112-21-58-96-53-25
107-8-2-95-105-85 71-47 23-70-3 12-92-115-K-53.
46-15-2-21-99-104-10-87-14-47-66-53 29-86 37-56-109-66
82-71-33-16 73-8 79-14 53-92-24 80-112 77-39 53-1-14
109-99-95 110-11-64.

82-24-41-103-95-71-58-104 107-36, 77 41-103-48 107

It took Derek and me two hours to write down all the letters that were under each number. When we were finished, this is what we had:

We are in France. Unable to use wireless.
Direction finding devices have located most of
them. Also unknown double agent in ranks.
Letters to you via courier and guides to
Portugal as safe alternative. Butterfly setting up
contacts and safe houses in Lyons. Bear has set
up office to falsify papers and plan escape
routes. B and B will be taking four children to
Spanish border in two weeks. Arrangements on
that side to be set up by SOE and COI.
       Standing by, B and B

There, sitting on my bed in the widow's peak room at the top of the house with the wind pounding on the windows and the moon frowning and flying through the clouds, I was to discover and to understand that my parents, Winnie and Danny, were British intelligence agents, having dropped into occupied France by parachute or boat, working against the Nazis under cover and in secret. My mum was the Butterfly and my dad was the Bear. And I cried that night in front of Derek and he cried a little too for me. I cried because I feared for my parents. I cried because I longed for them. I cried because I was angry at my parents for leaving me. And I cried because I was very, very proud of them.

★ *Forty-Eight* ★

It took Derek and me several days to decode all the other letters from the Bear and the Butterfly. We wrote them out in order. We read them over and over again. "We probably won't ever be able to understand the parts that seem to be a code within the code," said Derek. I nodded quietly.

Letter #2:

Butterfly and Bear housing 5 downed RAF pilots. Creating papers and passports. Arrange for passage from Portugal. Please send funds to Dr. R and departure dates. Magnolia wind and Mute Swan circuit.

Bear

Letter #3:

Butterfly back from Lyons. Has met American agent Delphine and has been asked to send word to SOE she needs some new

*bearings at the articulation where her wooden
leg meets the foot. No prosthetist in Lyons. Also
send new radio tubes for piano player in Green
Heart circuit. Have intercepted and decoded
German orders to move Le Garcon and Le Fou
to smaller prison in Limoges. Working on escape
plans. Nov 14. Code ABZ and awaiting lake
gardenia.*

Bear

Letter #4:

*Met "the Priest." Please check background.
Courier to send film from German factory where
Butterfly is employed. Should arrive by July 16.
Have collected ration books, stamps, and seals for
forgers. Send delivery instructions. Mute Swan
circuit alert. Code A.*

Bear

Letter #5:

*Guide G to walk 5 more children over the
Pyrenees. Butterfly staying in convent in
Aubeterre until G's arrival. Paperwork in place.
Awaiting drop of clothing and shoes for downed*

RAF. Gestapo has got the Monkey. Hoping for silence.

Bear and Butterfly

Letter #6:

Children have arrived in Portugal. Butterfly courier for Maquis in mountains till yesterday. Back with two more RAF needing papers. Direction finding devices have picked up Pierre's piano. Send replacement.

B and B

★ Forty-Nine ★

I was never to think of butterflies in the same way again. The yellow swallowtails and the migrating orange monarchs came to the spent rosebushes by the porch that late autumn, and because winter was nearing, I wanted to reach out for them. I wanted to catch them and bring them in the house and feed them, but of course they were better off left alone. Perhaps that was true too of Winnie and Danny. They were better off left to be the Bear and the Butterfly. It was wrong of Derek and me to intrude. They were doing important things. They were in France working behind the scenes and they were helping all kinds of people: downed English pilots, children, members of the Resistance, other agents, wireless operators. But the Gestapo had caught the Monkey. Who was the Monkey and what did that mean?

I looked out at the sea and I felt ashamed that I was doing nothing and that I was here longing for them to come home. Instead, all along, I should have been pleased that my parents were doing something extraordinary, even if it meant I would be lonely for them. But now their silence seemed larger, wider, darker.

And then I thought of Uncle Gideon and how I had been rather wrong about him, doubting and worrying about what he was doing, why he had been keeping all this from me, when all along, he had been waiting for Winnie and Danny's letters and transmitting the messages for them, probably making telephone calls for them, helping them, helping the people Winnie and Danny were helping. He had been going out to Peace Island all alone and climbing that old staircase to the top of the lighthouse to send word for them. And the friend from Washington, Mr. Donovan, must have known about their work. He must have been a part of their arrangements. He must have come to advise Uncle Gideon. Perhaps he even came to get the roll of film.

I had been so wrong about my uncle. And he had been such a good teacher. I thought I would hate being in an American school and having my uncle for a teacher, but I had actually liked it. Mr. Bathtub was quite dramatic as a teacher. Once, he even stood on his head to demonstrate a point during science class. And the way he taught math was rather inspiring. He had us all get up and be numbers and get added and subtracted and divided into each other, and we made lots of jokes and got awfully silly. I had noticed recently my own improvement with numbers.

Through all that, I had been doubting Uncle Gideon. I should have thought more of his loving and losing my Winnie. He had given up playing the piano because he had been hurt by her. He lost her to his brother, Danny, of all people, the one who always beat him at all the races, the one who always threw his rock farther, the one who always hit the ball harder.

The Gram said Uncle Gideon had something that Danny would never have, really. What was it? What did Gideon have that was a blessing in disguise? It seemed my stay in Bottlebay, Maine, was still to be lost in fog and mist, like that familiar fog that rolled in here every morning. Sometimes when I woke up, I couldn't see the ocean for the mist, and everything was hidden as if in a strange, complicated dream.

Now that I had an answer about Winnie and Danny, I felt the worse for it, as if I might break apart like the SS *Athenia* that cracked and shattered and sank to the bottom of the ocean when it was hit by Nazi torpe-does on the way to America.

I decided to go down on the beach and make a chair out of sand. It was chilly and windy and I had to wear a coat and mittens. I sat there in my sand chair on the beach and I stared at the water all afternoon.

★ *Fifty* ★

I shall never forget December 1, 1941. It was a cold day and our first snowfall. The windows in my tower room were iced over from the sleety snow that fell that day. I was sitting up in bed, not wanting to get out onto the chilly floor. But whenever it snows, I get a feeling of Christmas, and there it was all through the air in my gray tower room. Then I heard the doorbell ring at the kitchen door downstairs, the door nearest the driveway and away from the sea. That bell only worked sometimes when you poked and punched it, but when it did work, it was quite loud and jarring. "I'll get it," called Aunt Miami. Then I heard her rip down the stairs.

"A herd of buffalo could have done that more quietly," called The Gram from her bedroom. I heard doors opening and snapping shut and voices in the back hall.

Of course I was out of bed in a flash and dressed and halfway down the stairs when Auntie Miami called up, "Felicity Budwig Bathburn, you've gotten a letter. A real letter. Bob has kindly brought it right to the door."

Derek came screeching round the corner from the

parlor and nearly collided with me, and Uncle Gideon emerged from the library, looking hopeful with his glasses propped up on his head.

We all pushed into the kitchen, where Mr. Henley was standing in his snowy winter gear, a blue woolen cap, matching woolen jacket, his cheeks red with cold. "Look, Fliss," said Aunt Miami, "Bob's got a letter for you. Take it. Open it." She smiled at Mr. Henley and he smiled at her.

I stepped towards him praying it was a letter from Europe, hoping Winnie and Danny had finally sent me a Christmas card or a note. I reached out and took the long, white envelope. It was addressed to me and came from Washington, DC. I quickly opened it with the letter opener that Uncle Gideon had on hand. "Don't tear the return address," he said, putting on his glasses to see the envelope better.

Inside was a lovely letter on cream-colored stationery. I unfolded it quickly and read:

Dear Miss Felicity Bathburn Budwig,

Thank you for your charming letter. I receive letters from many youngsters, but yours particularly touched me. I always enjoy hearing from British children and it was pleasant indeed to hear you approve of my helping your country. When I speak to Mr. Churchill, I will indeed give him your regards and of course your secret will remain safe with me.

Very sincerely yours,

President Franklin Roosevelt

The president of the United States had written to *me*. All that afternoon in spite of everything, I walked on a pink cloud. Nothing could touch me. I floated from room to room. I played a round of Parcheesi with Uncle Gideon and almost won. And then Aunt Miami and I formed a team and beat him at Hearts. I practically sailed to rehearsals with Aunt Miami. But all the while too, Miami and Derek and Gideon pestered me.

"What's the secret President Roosevelt mentioned?" Miami said.

"Come on, Flissy, you can tell *me*," said Derek.

"Be a good sport, Fliss, spill the beans. What's the secret?" said Uncle Gideon.

And all I could do was say, "No. I just can't say. It's a secret."

I took the letter with me to rehearsals. The gold seal on the stationery seemed to shimmer. The letter got passed round the room. Even Mrs. Boxman saw it, and soon everyone, everyone, even Mrs. Fudge and Mr. Henley and the Balancing Bottlebay Boys and the group that would be singing "Say Au Revoir But Not Good-bye," *everyone* wanted to know what secret I shared with the president of the United States. But I just shook my head and said, "No, I can't. I won't." And I didn't.

We were just taking a break. Mrs. Fudge had brought in a key lime pie and we were all sitting at the table eating the pie, when Mrs. Boxman said, "Oh tra la la, we are going to have the best variety show this town has ever seen! I'm just so pleased with all of you. The show is almost perfect, but I do want to finish with a child singing. That will offer something forward looking for this Christmas season. Do you know a young person who can sing while I play the piano?"

Derek's good arm shot up and it was a long, strong arm that no one could miss. "Yes, Derek?" said Mrs. Boxman.

"Flissy. Our Flissy can sing. She sings all the time," he said.

And then I said, "I do sing Christmas carols, actually."

And Mrs. Boxman said, "Ah. Could you sing while I play the piano?"

"Yes," I said. "I think I can. What should I sing? 'Once in Royal David's City'?"

"No, Flissy," said Derek. "Sing 'I Think of You,' my favorite song. She knows all the words."

Mrs. Boxman looked pleased. "Oh, isn't that an old jazz song?" Mrs. Boxman said, sweeping over to the piano. I looked at Derek and then I looked at Aunt Miami and then the three of us followed Mrs. Boxman and stood together in a small widening circle round the piano.

So it was on December 1, 1941, at eight o'clock in the evening that I was recruited into the Bottlebay Women's Club Variety Show at the town hall in Bottlebay, Maine, United States of America, and it was on that very day too that I had received a genuine letter from President Franklin Delano Roosevelt.

As we were leaving the hall and heading out into the cold, with me sandwiched between Miami and Derek, someone called out in the darkness, "Hey, Flissy Bathburn, next time you talk to the Prez, tell him I said hello."

★ ☆ ★

Upon arriving home in the car that night, I noticed that the Bathburn house seemed to glow. So many lights were on in so many rooms all at once that it had a sort of warm jack-o'-lantern look to it. It seemed then like a great luminous beacon standing up high on the dark point, taking the wind on easily.

As I approached the back door, I was making up my mind about something again and so I walked quickly though the kitchen and on to the library. Uncle Gideon was writing at his desk in the corner. I walked over to the piano and I laid my hands on the lid.

Uncle Gideon looked up. "Hello, Flissy," he said, "what are you doing?"

"I'm here to ask you something. I am supposed to sing at the town hall and I was wondering if, I mean, I think it would be ever so lovely if you would, if you could, um, accompany me on the piano that night?"

"Oh, you do, do you?" he said.

"Pretty please? Winnie always said we *must* follow the things we are meant to do at *all* costs."

"She would say that," he said.

"I think your students at Babbington El might benefit from hearing you play," I said. "Truly."

"Oh, Flissy," he said, "I can't."

"Why not?" I said.

"Because," he said, "just because. I just can't."

★ *Fifty-One* ★

The next day, I took the letter from President Roosevelt to school. Uncle Gideon helped me frame it and we showed it to the librarian, who hugged me when she saw it. Everywhere we went, someone came rushing over to congratulate us. Mr. Bathtub and I went round to every class and showed the letter. We talked about Winston Churchill and Franklin Roosevelt. We even fashioned a kind of conversation between the two, which everyone thought was ever so interesting and a bit funny. Mr. Bathtub and I were rather a famous team all that day.

And so the Christmas season began with its extra week of shopping and the wonderful letter from Washington and "I Think of You" that I sang under my breath with every step I took. I tried not to look out across the sea and think of Winnie and Danny and what they were doing. I tried not to think about the German factory where Winnie was working. I tried not to think of Danny in his hidden office, making false passports. I tried not to think of the lines of downed RAF pilots in hiding, waiting to be smuggled back to England and I tried not to think about the letters that hadn't arrived. I pulled my curtains shut against it. Every time any of it floated into my mind, I tried to think of something else.

I thought instead about Christmas and the American Santa Claus and wondered if the British Father Christmas was the very same man. Bottlebay had already put up its town Christmas tree, and all the shops had pretty tinsel and candles in the windows. I knew Auntie Miami wanted a pair of nylons for Christmas, stockings that were not made of silk anymore and were cheaper. It was the newest rage and they were hard to come by. I was hoping I could find some for her. I was making my secret Christmas list in the dining room while Derek and Uncle Gideon and I listened to Sammy Kaye's *Sunday Serenade* on the radio.

Then, as soon as the show was over, a news bulletin broke in. *"From the NBC newsroom in New York, President Roosevelt said in a statement today that the Japanese have attacked Pearl Harbor in Hawaii from the air."* Uncle Gideon turned up the radio. *"There will be more reports later as news comes in."*

"That's it?" said Uncle Gideon. "Nothing more?" And then it cut to the next program.

"That's it?" said Uncle Gideon again. "My God. They've attacked us. Now it's done. We're at war. It's done.

That seals the deal. America is at war." And he fell back into the fat, green stuffed chair in the corner and he put his fingers over his eyes to hold them tight so that no tears would fall.

I believe Uncle Gideon sat by the radio all afternoon and he stayed up most of the night waiting for reports to come in. He seemed very tired the next day at school and his hair looked rather messy. He brought his radio to class and at twelve fifteen, President Roosevelt made his speech to Congress declaring war on Japan, and at the John E. Babbington Elementary School, Mr. Bathtub's sixth-grade class heard every word.

★ Fifty-Two ★

"The prime minister of your country is thankful we've joined the war and he says he's fond of President Roosevelt. It's in today's paper," said Derek.

"Oh, you mean Winston," I said. "Yes, I do think he's quite pleased with Franklin."

Derek and I were walking along the beach in the cold, heading away from the jetty and down towards the White Whale Inn. In the next few days after Japan had attacked Pearl Harbor, Germany had declared war on the United States as well.

I buttoned up my coat against the wind and followed Derek. He had a blue and gray wool scarf wrapped round his neck. He had borrowed it from Uncle Gideon. It made him look for a moment like a British schoolboy, a posh one who went to Eton like Jillian Osgood's older brother. And that gave me a smashing idea for a Christmas present for Derek. Since there were two weeks left, I was going to try to knit him a scarf.

We kept on going down the beach, and as we

walked, the old wooden hotel seemed to float towards us like an enormous abandoned ship. "Derek," I said quietly, "we haven't received any letters from the Bear and the Butterfly for a very long time. Do you think it means anything?"

"I don't know, Flissy. I don't know," said Derek.

"Do you think the bombers will come here soon? Do you think we will have to get blackout curtains as well?"

"Don't know," said Derek again. We were both very quiet for a moment. "I have thought a lot about those letters, and from all I have gathered, I think your mother has saved a lot of children in France, children who would have otherwise been killed."

"Oh," I said and I closed my eyes. "I told you my Winnie is lovely."

"And Gideon does some things too. When I was in his study, there were papers on the desk that I understand better now. I think he wires information from Peace Island to ships at sea, like the convoys on the way to England. I'm guessing he works for Mr. Donovan, who works for the president of the United States."

"I know, Derek," I said. "And how lovely that he has been doing all that. And I've been wrong and mean." I closed my eyes again because the wind was making terrible tears that flew out and away behind me.

"And while we're on the subject of questions, what's the secret you told President Roosevelt?" Derek said, knocking his foot against mine.

I looked at him for a moment, at his pale, freckled face full of new cheer. The secret was in my heart and it *wanted* to break out. It wanted to. I could feel it, but instead of saying a word, I started to run, ripping and leaping towards the White Whale Inn. And Derek chased me.

We both ran up on the porch and tried to peer in the windows. Through a crack in one of the curtains, we could see white sheets draped over chairs and sofas, everything shrouded and ghostlike.

I watched Derek as he looked here and there. I thought all the while to myself that he seemed very changed since we had decoded the letters from Winnie and Danny. He had really transformed in some quiet way. I wasn't sure yet how or why.

Through another window, I could see down the hall into part of the dining room. I pushed to see more, but it was impossible. Whatever else was there, I had to imagine. It was that way too with the Bathburns. There were pieces, parts of the picture I understood, but much was still shrouded as if covered in white sheets for winter. Like what was the blessing in disguise that The Gram had talked about, and when would we hear from Winnie and Danny again? And how could the sky be so blue when America was now at war?

★ Fifty-Three ★

Some of my questions were to be answered sooner than I thought. A week before Christmas, we put up a tree in the parlor. Mr. Henley brought it to us one Saturday and it was so tall it touched the ceiling. It really was quite magnificent. He called it a great northern white pine and it filled the house with the smell of pinesap. Aunt Miami and Mr. Henley practiced their lines in the library and I could often hear "Romeo, Romeo, wherefore art thou Romeo?" drift through the hall. It carried with it now so many layers of meaning.

I made a Christmas card for Winnie and Danny. I drew a picture of a bear and a butterfly and a Christmas tree. On the front, it said, "*Merry Christmas, Winnie and Danny*" and inside I wrote *HOPE* in great big letters. I put it in the box under my bed.

The Gram had been upstairs in her room sewing all month. Late into the night, I could hear the sewing machine buzzing along, and by day, it pounded above us when we were in the library.

On the evening of December eighteenth, I went up to my room to my closet and I reached under the yellow suitcase and got out the letter written from Winnie to Gideon. It was a bit wrinkled, but unopened, and I put it in my skirt pocket and went downstairs. Uncle Gideon was just coming up the stairs as I was going down them and so we stopped on the same step, and Uncle Gideon said one more time, "Flissy, I'm still waiting for a letter from Europe. I've been waiting and waiting and waiting. You are sure you haven't seen anything?"

"No," I said. "I haven't."

"It's very important," he said. "If you did see a letter, you would tell me, of course."

"I know what those letters are," I said. "Derek and I figured out the code. We know."

Uncle Gideon seemed quite startled for a moment and then he looked very sadly at me for a long time. He didn't say anything. Finally, he lowered his eyes. "It doesn't have to mean the worst, Flissy. It could be many things. Perhaps our ally in the postal system in Portugal changed jobs, for instance." We both sat down on the same step. "It could just be a break in any one of the many links. Bill Donovan in Washington and the Office of the COI has said we must sit tight."

I looked down at my hands and saw the letter lying in my lap, but it seemed now blurry and so far away, and I felt as if I could barely reach down to pick it up.

"What's this letter, Flissy?" said Uncle Gideon.

"It's from Winnie to you," I said. "It was written in May when I first arrived. Winnie asked me to keep it till now, a week before Christmas. She said not to open it."

Uncle Gideon reached out for the letter as if it were a rose. His hands lightly trembled. Then the letter lay in his palm like a small white bird resting. He closed his eyes and held the letter carefully, gently, not opening it and not moving. "She gave you this for *me*?" he said. His voice sounded crumbly and dark and gentle all at the same time.

"Yes," I said. "Open it."

"You know, Fliss, I haven't said this before and I probably won't say it again," he said, looking at me now, "but you do look so much like your mother. No, you really do."

"I do?" I said. "I never thought about that."

"Your mother is a great idealist. And it's a rather dark world right now, Fliss."

"I know," I said.

"I think you might be a bit of an idealist too, and that's not a bad thing," said Uncle Gideon.

"Are you going to open the letter?" I said.

"Yes," he said, closing his eyes again and nodding his head. "Yes, of course." And he began pulling at the envelope with the greatest of care, both of us watching his fingers on the white paper. Then, sitting on the tenth step halfway down to the front door, we read the letter. It said:

Dearest Gideon,

I am writing this on the porch while you and Danny go off together to Peace Island. Please know that I still cherish my time with you. I never intended to hurt you. But what happened could not be prevented or stopped or changed. It was too overpowering and thus inevitable. Of course a part of me will always remember you. Can you ever forgive me? Can you ever forgive Danny? When you read this, if you have not heard from us as of mid-November, when, as you know, we will be part of a certain maneuver, please tell my little Felicity everything. Everything.

Love,

Winnie

Uncle Gideon folded the letter, sandwiched it between his two hands, and looked down at me.

"I already know everything," I said. "We cracked the code. We read the letters. I know everything."

"No," said Uncle Gideon, "there's something else you do not know. Something extremely important. Have you ever wondered why we both have the same reddish-brown hair or why we both like to read Frances Hodgson Burnett while eating toffee or how it is that we both have just the right shaped head and sense of balance to stand with some ease on our heads? Have you ever wondered?"

"No, actually, I haven't," I said.

"Well, perhaps you should. You knew that I was once married to your mother."

"Yes, I did."

"And that I loved her very dearly."

"Yes."

"Oh, Flissy. Oh, Flissy. Don't you know? Don't you know? You are not my niece at all, you are my own little daughter. I'm your father and *you* are my own little daughter," he said and he hugged me and he cried. We both sat there on the tenth step, crying together.

"You are my father?" I said.

"How long, how long I have waited," he said then, "to tell you and to have you home here with me finally where you belong."

★ ☆ ★

Where I belong. Where I belong. Where I belong. Those words seemed to rock me to sleep in my tower room. Those words seemed to warm me as I ran in the wind along the shore or as I went through the kitchen to grab a cookie from the just-for-Sunday cookie jar. *Where I belong. Where I belong. Where I belong.*

I was the blessing in disguise. It was *me*. That evening and the days that followed, I was to unravel and understand it all, to untangle it all like something knitted the wrong way. I was to unravel it and to knit it back the right way, just as I knitted Derek's Christmas scarf. Knit one, pearl one. Knit two, pearl two. My Danny was my uncle, not my father, and Uncle Gideon was not my uncle but my father. Winnie and Gideon had been married in England for three months and I was conceived then. I was Gideon's child. I had the same reddish-brown hair. We both liked to read. *I* was his blessing in disguise. I belonged somewhere. I belonged somewhere. I belonged *here*.

★ *Fifty-Four* ★

Perhaps it was something like wearing new shoes or having a completely new way of fixing your hair or having a new name or going to a new school or looking in the mirror and having a completely different air about you. Everything was changed. And I needed time to let it all sift through me like beach sand as it falls through your fingers when you try to hold it in your hand.

Derek said to me when I told him about it later, "I always felt I was a stand-in, a replacement for somebody or something, and now I see, Flissy, it was you. It was you I was standing in for. *That's* why we have the same birthday. *That's* why and how I came to live here. And it was a lucky thing for me, you know that?"

"It's nice, isn't it, having the same birthday. Don't you think?" I said.

While everything sifted through me, I knitted. I was working on Derek's scarf secretly every chance I got. Every stitch I took, I thought about belonging, belonging, belonging.

Just before Christmas and one day before our performance at the town hall in Bottlebay, I finished the scarf and I put the fringe on the ends of it. I had folded it up and tucked it in red tissue paper. I was sitting on Miami's bed with her while we wrapped presents and we were handing the scissors and the tape back and forth. The tape was made of brown paper and I had to lick the back to make it sticky.

There was a Glenn Miller big band song playing on the radio downstairs. Derek had turned up the music loud again. "I *must* dance to this one," Aunt Miami said, and she dropped the scissors on the bed and circled out of the room.

I went to the top of the stairs to watch her and she'd already found a willing partner. My father. They were swirling through the hall and into the parlor and then back through the hall and into the dining room. "We have to live for the moment, Flissy," called Miami. "After all, America is in the war now. And who knows what will happen." The saxophones and horns played through the house. *I* was the blessing in disguise. All along it was *me*.

"Do you have any tape?" said Derek, coming out of his room with a piece of wrapping paper and a small box in his hands.

"There is some in here in Auntie's room," I said. He followed me into the room.

"So Miami and Gideon are downstairs cutting a rug," said Derek. "It's nice."

The music stopped for a moment and then we could hear an announcement urging civilians to report for volunteer duty. After that, there was an ad for Carter's Little Liver Pills. Derek sat with me on Miami's bed and cut off a piece of wrapping paper and started to wrap up the small box with his one hand, which wasn't terribly easy. "About me not being able to enlist someday, I've decided on something. I've thought of something interesting, Flissy. Something that's changed everything."

"What is it, Derek?" I said.

He didn't answer me for a minute. "I realized it when I read the letters from your Winnie and Danny. I realized it when I read about the agent with the wooden leg. That's when I realized it, Fliss. You can have a handicap and still work for the war and the government. If that person with a handicap should want to become an intelligence agent, it would be possible, acceptable, even welcome. I have talked with Gideon about it, and when I am a little older, *that* is what I am going to do, Flissy. That is what my work will be."

I smiled at him, all the while thinking that he was ever so brave and ever so sweet and ever so lovely. Then he said, "It's nice to see Miami dancing. It's nice for Gideon too. You know, Fliss, like I said before, you stirred up the soup around here. In a good way."

"I did?" I said.

"Yes, you did," he said. "You know, Flissy..." He paused. "Um. I have a secret too. I didn't write to the president about it yet, but I might."

"Oh, *you* have a secret?" I said, looking up at him. "Is it a nice secret or a mean secret?"

"It's a nice secret," he said.

"Oh, then tell me," I said, squeezing my eyes tightly and listening closely.

"If you tell me *your* secret first, I'll tell you mine," Derek said.

"When?" I said. "Now?"

"Well, not today and not tomorrow," he said, "but maybe the next day."

"Really?" I said.

"Possibly," he said. "Or the day after the day after tomorrow."

"Truly?" I said.

"Maybe. Perhaps," he said, smiling down at me.

Then he handed me the package he had wrapped. "This is for you, Flissy," he said. "I didn't want to give it to you on Christmas. I didn't want the others to see."

I reached out and took the present. I unwrapped it slowly. I took the lid off carefully. Inside, staring up at me, was the beautiful little tin soldier with the missing arm.

★ ☆ ★

The next morning, the sky was bright and cloudless. We had hot cocoa for breakfast, and the early light that fell through the windows in every room was clear. The air smelled of chocolate and maple syrup and oatmeal. I was standing in the kitchen, I think, when I heard the most beautiful melodic piano music. It rolled out of the library like the ocean rolling up on the shore. It thundered through the house, speaking, singing, calling, sobbing, laughing. Miami and Derek and The Gram and I stood in the hallway listening. My grandmother was crying. She was crouched over, trying not to, but there was nothing she could do about it. She seemed finally to relax, to uncurl, to unwind in tears. Miami shook her head at me and said, "You see, Gideon's good. He's good." Slowly, we opened the library door and went in and listened to the music streaming from my father's fingers on the piano, and he was looking at each of us, and all of him seemed somehow to be entwined in the music and all of him was pouring from the notes. I felt as if I was seeing him really for the first time. The music grew louder and then softer. It rolled and then it thundered, touching every wall and window, every corner of the Bathburn house. He nodded at me as he played and I knew then that he was going to accompany me on the piano when I sang tomorrow night. He didn't have to say one word. It was there quite clearly in my father's smile.

★ Fifty-Five ★

Two days before Christmas was the night of our performance. For dinner, The Gram made winter vegetable soup. Miami chopped the onions. Derek measured out the rice. And yes, I stirred the soup. Then after dinner, we got into the Packard, which almost didn't start, and we drove just after dark to the town hall. It was a bumpy, slippery ride, and the windscreen was icy and the back window couldn't be rolled up, so the wind was blowing in all over the place, but the cold didn't seem to bother me. I was holding a nice, fat hot water bottle that The Gram had filled for me before we left.

When we got to the town hall, there was a light snow falling. The sky was dark, and looking up through the snowflakes, I could see the little lights of stars shining so far away. Gideon said it was an unusual combination of snow and the Big and Little Dipper.

"Maybe it's a sign," said Gideon, putting his arm over The Gram's shoulder and squeezing Aunt Miami's hand for a minute. "Maybe we're going to win this war after all."

When we got to the town hall, there was an enormous Christmas wreath on the front door, covered with hundreds of tiny burning candles, and I felt suddenly nervous and scared to get up and sing the last song of the evening.

Already, there were many people sitting in the folding chairs, waiting for the show to begin. Derek and I and Gideon and The Gram sat in the front row while Auntie Miami went backstage. She had put her hair in bobby pin curlers the night before and now her hair fell in dark ringlets specially created for the part. As she waved to me, I thought she looked ever so full of grace and ease.

Soon the curtains parted and the scene from *Romeo and Juliet* began. Miami said those lines yet one more time, "Romeo, Romeo, wherefore art thou Romeo?" And the code came into my mind again and the journey my Winnie and Danny had gone on in France. "Romeo, Romeo, wherefore art thou Romeo? Deny thy father and refuse thy name, or, if thou wilt not, be but sworn my love, and I'll no longer be a Capulet." Those words yet again carrying with them all that sadness and loveliness. Gideon had said, "It doesn't have to mean the worst. It could be many things."

And then, like a mirage, Mr. Henley appeared onstage

and he looked at Juliet with such tenderness and love, it was hard to believe it was a play. It was so real. Mr. Henley almost seemed to tremble when he swore his love to Juliet. And my aunt Miami bloomed that night like a flower, like a rose, like a beautiful wild rose on a scrubby bush along the ocean.

At the end of the scene, Romeo and Juliet kissed and the crowd cheered and clapped and they stomped on the old wooden floor with their feet and asked for an encore. Then Aunt Miami and Mr. Henley seemed to be flying, lifting off the stage and sailing above us, rinsed in a dazzling moment, holding hands.

After that, Mrs. Paula Martin got onstage and played the ukulele, followed by the acrobatic Balancing Bottlebay Boys. Mrs. Fudge and her parrot sang, and then the Four Voices did "Say Au Revoir But Not Good-bye." And soon enough, the variety show was almost over and my turn was coming up. Derek touched my hand and said, "Break a leg, Flissy."

Then I went round to the backstage with my father and waited in the wings. I knew I was going to sing "I Think of You" for Winnie and Danny. I had been planning that. I also knew that I would be singing it for Derek. The makeup crew came by and put real lipstick on my lips and added rouge to my cheeks and the whole time they were working on me, I was making up my mind about something again.

I decided that night that I was going to send my Wink to Lily's little brother, Albert, in England. I knew he loved Wink dearly and needed him more than I did now, and besides, Wink had been neglected recently. How easy it was to get so busy with important things and neglect someone. But it didn't mean that you didn't love them. And after all, I was going to be twelve years old this January, and girls of twelve in the United States *never* carry bears around.

Thinking about all that made my being nervous go away and it made something else happen. Suddenly, as I was about to go onstage, suddenly like a wind washing over the ocean, suddenly I felt like a real part of Bottlebay, Maine. I felt like I was in a circle with everybody in the room near me, with Derek, Auntie Miami, The Gram, and my father, Gideon, AKA Mr. Bathtub, who would now need another new name altogether. Another new name. As The Gram had said, "A person can call their father by any name they like. It's your choice, Flissy."

Suddenly as I stood there, I sensed all the Bathburns close around me and I felt like I might be becoming a real true American and it felt super and warm and good. Then I remembered Danny saying to Winnie as she cried, "The Bathburns of Bottlebay will be a great gift for her, Winnie. The best gift you could give a child. The very best." And he was ever so right.

Then I went out and stood under the lights and sang "I Think of You," and my father played the piano. I sang,

When the clouds roll by
and the moon drifts through
When the haze is high
I think of you.
I think of you.

When the mist is sheer
and the shadows too
When the moon is spare
I think of you.
I think of you.

And all I could do was wait and hope and hope and hope that one day when the skies were clear of fighter planes and bombers, and the sea was free of U-boats and aircraft carriers and warships, that one day, I would see my Winnie and my Danny running towards me on the beach, stopped in midair, the sky hot and blue and quiet and the sea barely moving, like a beautiful still photograph.

Author's Note

Flissy Bathburn's story is fictional, but the historical incidents surrounding World War II in this book are true, with a few exceptions. In my story Flissy and Winnie and Danny crossed the ocean on the Cunard ocean liner the *Queen Anne* in 1941. This boat is fictional although based upon the great Cunard ocean liner the *Queen Elizabeth* and her secret maiden voyage in 1940 from England to the United States for safekeeping. The *Queen Elizabeth* was indeed painted entirely gray, including the portholes, so that no light would escape. And she did indeed zigzag silently across the ocean evading Nazi submarines.

Flissy's beloved Winnie and Danny, as well as Gideon Bathburn, were all intelligence agents working with the English office of espionage in London called the SOE (Special Operations Executive) and also with the newly developed American intelligence gathering agency called the COI (Coordinator of Information) under the direction of Gen. William J. Donovan, the man who visited the Bathburns in my book. In reality quite a few

British agents were women and some of them had children they left behind at home. There were a few husband and wife teams and sometimes romantic involvements among the agents. Many of these agents were beautiful and loved danger and intrigue. They were very brave and heroic and often died helping others.

In my story the agent with the wooden leg called Delphine as a code name was based on a real agent named Virginia Hall. She was an American who posed as a *New York Post* reporter in the Lyons region in France starting in 1941. At some point she did need word sent to America to get parts for her wooden leg which she couldn't obtain in Lyons, although Winnie and Danny's role in that story is fictional. Virginia Hall helped countless downed British RAF pilots and many other people get false papers and find escape routes. She also arranged for funds, obtained authentic-looking French clothing and shoes for their disguise, and provided other agents and downed pilots with safe houses. She even helped break some Resistance members out of prison.

There were unfortunately German sympathizers among the French who posed as part of the Resistance and who really worked for the Nazis. They turned in many Allied agents and blew the cover of many Resistance groups working all over France. One such agent was named Henri Déricourt. He worked in a very important position receiving Allied agents on the ground as they parachuted into central France. Many British agents and wireless operators were captured days later possibly because of this double agent. Although unproven, it appears he was responsible for destroying a major Resistance circuit called "Prosperous" and damaging other circuits.

The wireless operators were called "piano players" and it was a very dangerous job as the Nazis had direction finding devices that were often able to detect where the transmitters were. Once a wireless operator was caught, the Nazis used the same wireless machines and secret codes to send false messages back to the SOE in London. The messages often asked Britain for money, artillery, and other supplies. Sadly the SOE responded to these false messages by dropping in supplies and money that immediately fell into the hands of the Nazis.

I imagined while writing my story that Winnie and Danny had become aware of an important double agent posing as their circuit's wireless operator and so they planned to use an alternative route and method to get information to the COI and the SOE. They decided to send letters via courier through neutral Portugal as a safer alternative. The trip over the Pyrenees Mountains to neutral Spain and Portugal was the preferred route for smuggling British pilots back to England and many agents went back to London this way, including agent Virginia Hall when she escaped France finally by walking over the snowy Pyrenees, in spite of her wooden leg. Most airmail letters and packages going from Europe to the USA went from Lisbon, Portugal. These letters were all checked by a censor looking for letters containing sensitive information. I imagined that Danny, Gideon, and Winnie had an ally in the postal system in Portugal who stamped the letters with a "passed censor" stamp allowing the letters to go through unchecked.

I know that Britain and America worked together as a unit in their spy efforts starting in 1942, but in my story I imagined that officials in Washington like General Donovan at the COI began organizing and running spy operations in Europe in the spring of 1941 before the US joined the war. Actually, General Donovan did not begin planning such covert operations until a year later when he started the OSS. Therefore this part of my story is purely fictional. However President Roosevelt was very independent and interested in espionage and had sent Donovan to England in 1940 to learn all he could about organizing spy circuits, so this part of my story is actually quite possible.

I was a ten-year-old girl when I lived in England and went to school there in the late 1950s. The first time I was in London I was struck by the numerous piles of brick ruble still on many street corners where buildings had been bombed. Much of the detail of Flissy Bathburn's life in England comes directly from my firsthand 1950s experiences while living the life of a British girl.

Acknowledgements

Very special thanks to Rachel Griffiths, my editor, who is always sure and confident when I waver, and who has steered this project with great intelligence and enthusiasm, offering creative and inspiring suggestions that helped this book to become exactly what it is. Thank you!! A special thank-you also to Arthur Levine for his behind-the-scenes support and encouragement and kindness. In fact, thank you to all the people at Scholastic and Arthur A. Levine Books. I could not be happier! Thank you, Nikki Mutch!!! Thank you also to my friends who read this book for me early on: Susan Cole, child advocate lawyer and lecturer at Harvard Law School; Anne Corrigan, former British citizen now teaching at Mary Hogan Elementary School; my scientist friends Yvette Feig and Bob Murray; Kristy Carlson, avid reader; and my sister Marcia Croll, who always reads my books for me when I call up and say, "Quick! Read it overnight. I need to know what you think." And she does. And thank you to my ever encouraging mom, the poet Ruth Stone, who says the only books she reads are children's books, mine among them. Wow! And thank you to my husband and best friend David Carlson, who is always a part of all my books and as I am writing this now, I know he will read it over in a few minutes and tell me where I have misspelled or misplaced a stray or wandering word. We are all a team. I am forever grateful.

And a note of gratitude to these nonfiction books and authors who helped me understand Winnie and Danny's complicated world.

The Women Who Lived for Danger: Behind Enemy Lines During World War II by Marcus Binney. Harper Paperbacks, 2004.

The Wolves at the Door: The True Story of America's Greatest Female Spy by Judith L. Pearson. The Lyons Press, 2005.

Sisterhood of Spies: Women of the OSS by Elizabeth P. McIntosh. Naval Institute Press, 1998.

A Life in Secrets: Vera Atkins and the Missing Agents of World War II by Sarah Helm. Anchor Books, 2007.

Operatives, Spies, and Saboteurs: The Unknown Story of World War II's OSS by Patrick O'Donnell. Citadel Press Book, 2004.